"Is it time for my ...

Rosemary's voice was husky as she stretched in anticipation. Her torso lifted provocatively, and she watched Ryan's lips part.

"Not if you don't stop that," he said with a teasing smile.

His hands were warm as he stroked her body, fingertips to sensitive toes. Rosemary was melting when the tempo changed, when Ryan cupped her breasts, making her gasp. Yet only after he had nipped and tasted, to her complete frustration and pleasure, did she moan, "Ryan, please, I need you...."

Suddenly they were together, kissing, her tongue joining the rough velvet of his in a sensual duel....

THE AUTHOR

It was a good thing for Marion Smith Collins that her agent moved from Manhattan to Queens, because that gave her the starting point for this Temptation. Marion decided to write about a woman who uproots herself—and for the first time is surrounded by grass and flowers.

The author's own romantic spirit helps her to write. Only a romantic would take a double course load so she could finish college when her fiancé did! Marion now lives with her husband in Georgia.

Books by Marion Smith Collins

HARLEQUIN TEMPTATION
5—BY MUTUAL CONSENT
22—BY ANY OTHER NAME
35—THIS THING CALLED LOVE
49—ON THE SAFE SIDE
63—THIS TIME, THIS MOMENT

These books may be available at your local bookseller.

Don't miss any of our special offers. Write to us at the following address for information on our newest releases.

Harlequin Reader Service
P.O. Box 52040, Phoenix, AZ 85072-2040
Canadian address: P.O. Box 2800, Postal Station A,
5170 Yonge St., Willowdale, Ont. M2N 6J3

This Time, This Moment

MARION SMITH COLLINS

Harlequin Books

TORONTO • NEW YORK • LONDON
AMSTERDAM • PARIS • SYDNEY • HAMBURG
STOCKHOLM • ATHENS • TOKYO • MILAN

To Barbara and Ray Weddle,
who know what true friendship should be,
in theory and in practice.

To Johnny and Buffy Campbell,
whose visits are precious,
but they're so rare.

And with special thanks to Bob Evans,
vice-president of product development
for Wellco Carpet Corporation,
Calhoun, Georgia.
Bob is the opposite of the Charles character.

Published June 1985

ISBN 0-373-25163-7

1

ANY MINUTE NOW. *Ryan will be here any minute.* Rosemary Addison felt anticipation sing through her veins. Recessed lighting reflected on her unbound raven hair as she hovered over the table with uncharacteristic nervousness, straightening napkins and silver flatwear. Two place settings were perfectly aligned.

Ashtray. A snap of her fingers broke the silence in the apartment. She needed an ashtray, unless Ryan had kept to his resolution to stop smoking. She pivoted, silk rustling against her knees, and crossed the room to push aside the high-gloss panels, revealing a small wet bar. As she reached into a lower cabinet where the ashtrays were kept, she automatically inventoried the liquor supply again. Crystal decanters with engraved silver necklaces stood in a row—Scotch before dinner for Ryan, a red vermouth or sherry for her, Drambuie afterward—had she forgotten anything?

Chimes pealed, and Rosemary was so startled that the ashtray slipped from her fingers to bounce softly on the rug. Damn! This was senseless. Retrieving it hastily, she threatened its delicacy once more by slamming it against the bar counter. Why should she be nervous about seeing an old friend like Ryan, she wondered disgustedly. Why should she be nervous about meeting anyone?

She marched to the door. Just before reaching for the knob, however, she twitched at the tiny mandarin collar of her cherry-red dress, adjusted the obi sash around her narrow waist and licked her lips.

Swinging the door wide, she held out her hands to the large, immaculately dressed man who stood there. "Ryan," she said softly. Her happiness at seeing him was reflected in her eyes, giving them an extra sparkle.

Ryan Tarleton caught her hands in his warm grasp. His gaze settled on her for a moment before he pulled her forward for a light kiss. The pleasant essence of rich cologne lingered on him. The brush of his mustache and the clean, familiar smell of him were as welcome as the affectionate arm across her shoulders.

"Rosie. You're looking as beautiful as ever," he declared fondly. Words that might have been a meaningless social greeting from some of her friends were patently sincere when spoken by Ryan.

Rosemary marveled that after all these years, his deep, lazy drawl was still tempered with an Ivy League inflection, the result of college and graduate-school years spent at Harvard. Though she saw Ryan only four or five times a year when he had to be in the city on business, her pleasure in his company never diminished. There was no awkwardness between them, often the case with friends whose meetings are infrequent.

"Thanks. You look well, too."

Ryan was always perfectly groomed yet never gave the appearance of having been punched from a mold, as so many sophisticated men did. His tailored suit was a shade of gray just darker than his eyes. The Southern sun had tanned the skin of his hands and face, providing a contrast to the pristine white cuffs and collar of his shirt. His hair was the color of burned toast and had been cut to lie in careless perfection. He was an imposing figure at six foot three, and though he never seemed dictatorial, Rosemary knew his will was as solid as his square jawline.

"I'm glad you're here," she added, hoping he wouldn't catch the note of feverishness she heard in her voice as she moved into his arms for a hug. "I've missed you." She allowed her head to rest for a minute on his broad chest.

The statement was absolutely true. In the four months since his last visit, she'd missed him more than ever before—his strength, his slow easy manner, his patience with what he teasingly called her "artistic temperament," which was admittedly difficult to bear at times.

A quick intake of breath above her head warned her that he hadn't failed to recognize her unusual agitation. Rosemary lifted her head and gave him a bright smile. "Four months is a long time between visits. You usually come more often."

He wasn't fooled. His dark brows drew together in an expression of concern. "Is something wrong, Rosie?" Ryan asked gently, his arms tightening around her.

She almost let go of the hysterical laugh that bubbled in her throat and lifted her fingers to his freshly shaved cheek, unable to resist touching another warm human being. "Nothing's wrong, Ryan," she lied. Taking a step that freed her from his embrace, she gestured with her hand. "Come inside."

Ryan moved past Rosemary into the living room and stood, silently looking around at all the reflective surfaces—chrome, glass, crystal, shimmery mirrors, tiny sparks of light from the chandelier— starkly contemporary and utterly chic. The slow survey allowed him time to think, but it didn't settle his misgivings. She had given up her own smaller apartment for the sleek Fifth Avenue pied- à-terre that had been her father's home before his death. This was Ryan's first visit since she'd moved.

The disturbing fears that had budded in him as a result of Rosemary's nervous greeting grew. He truly cared about her, as only a friend of long- standing could care. Something serious had hap- pened to her. She had lost weight since he'd last seen her, and even a few pounds less on her slender frame was too much. The signs of agitation disturbed him, too. Her restless hands, her darting gaze, the voice an octave higher than usual—all were so unlike Rosemary. And this room! It had all the warmth of an Eskimo's refrigerator.

Rosemary looked beyond Ryan to the room. Seen through his eyes, it made her uneasy. There was something missing. How strange that she hadn't noticed it before. The apartment had been a perfect setting for her sophisticated father. She closed the door, leaned against it and transferred her gaze to Ryan's broad back. "How do you like it?" she tried to ask casually.

Ryan glanced back, meeting her eyes briefly; his narrowed. "What have you done with your furniture?" he asked finally, turning again to view the room.

"Everything's in storage. I decided I needed a change." Rosemary's hand swept the air carelessly while she waited for his reaction. Approaching him to stand just behind his shoulder, she went on, "All those antiques, that tradition, was weighty."

Ryan unbuttoned the jacket of his dark suit and shoved his hands into his pockets. He frowned as he looked over his shoulder once more, into the deep blue of her eyes.

She couldn't read his thoughts, but that wasn't unusual. Ryan frequently kept his inner feelings to himself, especially if they concerned something he didn't approve of. No amount of cajoling would free those feelings, either, until he was ready.

He didn't speak for a moment; then he shrugged.

"I guess I'm just surprised. I always liked your apartment, and I thought you'd move your own furniture with you. But if you're comfortable..."

She laughed lightly. "Surely you can be more honest than that. Sit down. I'll fix you a drink. Scotch?" She moved toward the bar.

"Please."

Out of one corner of an eye she watched as he carefully lowered himself onto a puffy, suede couch. Returning with their drinks, she slid gracefully into one of two upright chairs at right angles to the sofa. "Really, now," she pressed. "What do you think?"

Staring into his glass, Ryan shook his head and took a swallow before he answered. "You don't want to know," he said, his mouth curving into a derisive half smile.

Rosemary sat back in her chair, linking her hands around her own stemmed glass. "Obviously you don't approve."

"Is my opinion so important?" His mustache quirked at one corner of the well-shaped mouth. "I'll only see it a couple of times a year. You're the one who has to live with it every day."

"I know, but I still value your opinion. You're my friend."

He dropped his eyes, laughing harshly. "I wouldn't be your friend for long if I told you what I thought about this room, but I'd love to hear how a psychologist would interpret all these hard, reflective surfaces."

"A psychologist?" she repeated blankly. Rosemary's heart lurched. She couldn't look away from the expression in his eyes. Was it accusatory? Did the apartment give the impression of self-indulgence? "Actually, the place is beginning to grow on me." She swallowed. "I've been very lonely since father died. It's comforting to live among his things, where he lived."

The effect on him was instantaneous. "Lonely? Dammit, Rosie...!" His hand jerked involuntarily, sloshing a few drops of the drink over his fingers. He blotted the moisture with a tiny cocktail napkin. The scrap of linen was too small and too starched to be of any effect, but the action gave him a minute to take in the impact of her speech. In the five years since he'd known her, he'd never heard her admit to loneliness. "When I was here four months ago you didn't seem lonely."

She remembered the night well. His visit had coincided with her twenty-ninth birthday, and he'd taken her out to celebrate. They had dined at one of Manhattan's most elegant spots; afterward dancing and then playing tourist, riding in a hansom cab through the park. It had been a wonderful birthday, one she would always remember happily. Soon after he'd left the restlessness had begun.

"We had a good time that night, didn't we?"

"I never thought I'd get you into a hansom cab." He chuckled. "You always said those rides were for tourists."

"Actually it was shortly after you left that this all began."

Ryan was suddenly very still. For the first time there was honest sadness in her voice. Now maybe they were getting to the root of the problem, and maybe he could find a way to help. "Tell me about it," he urged quietly.

Rosemary tightened her fingers around the glass and searched the depths of the amber liquid as though the answer could be found there.

She paused to take a sip of the dry sherry. The heavy wine had a smooth, fortifying taste. "I had hoped this move would jolt me out of the doldrums, and it did help for a while." She laughed self-mockingly. "I was content for almost a month."

The chimes of the doorbell innocently pierced the silence following her words. Rosemary's head swung to the door and then back at him. "I'm not expecting anyone."

"I'll get it. I asked Paxton Norwood, my CEO, to drop some papers by." Ryan struggled out of the plushy depths of the sofa.

Chief Executive Officer, she correctly interpreted. She had never met the man, but she'd heard about him from Ryan. "Would you like to ask him in?"

"Not tonight, and remind me not to sit there again," he muttered testily as his long legs took him across the floor. There was a short conversation behind her, and soon he was back, dropping a manila file folder on the coffee table. He picked up his drink and stood glaring down at the sofa accusingly. "My God, Rosie, where in the hell did your father get that thing?"

She laughed and named a showroom well-known for its bizarre attitude toward furniture design.

"That's better," Ryan said enigmatically, but he grinned back.

"What is?"

"That's the first real smile you've given me since I walked in that door." Taking the upright chair beside her, he turned slightly, crossing one ankle over his knee, and took a swallow of his drink. He lifted the glass to the light, studying it before he spoke again. "Are you going to tell me what else is bothering you?"

"Probably, but not right now." She smiled to take the sting from her words. For some reason she needed to gain just a bit more time before elaborating.

"The unflappable Ms Addison seems very uptight tonight."

"You're right, of course. You always are— Okay, maybe it will help to tell you. I've been...restless for months." Her smile tilted sadly. "And missing father, of course. It's been just the two of us for so long. If my mother had lived long enough for me to have at least a memory..."

Ryan's glance was skeptical. "But that's not all of the problem."

"No," she admitted. Rosemary surged to her feet and crossed the room to the window. Setting her glass on the sill, she hugged her arms around her, staring out; the stunning view of Central Park was lost on her. She had lived a really full twenty-nine years, the last ten oriented toward achievement. "I have everything I've ever strived for—everything I've ever wanted. I can pick and choose the projects I work on and command almost any fee for my designs. I've worked hard as hell to get where I am, but now that I'm here, I'm...confused and empty, Ryan." After all that had gone before, after aspiration and ambition had been fulfilled, after talent had been developed to attain success, she was just plain empty.

She turned back to him, forcing a laugh. "I can't ever remember being this confused before, and I don't like it." Her voice was rising, but she couldn't seem to control the pitch. "What's wrong with me? I feel as though any minute I might splinter into pieces and scatter, and there would be nothing of substance to show that I'd been here at all."

Ryan's heart went out to her as he watched from across the room. He sensed that for the first time in her life Rosemary Addison felt as delicate as she looked. She was turned half away from him, but he could see the fragile bone structure of her cheek, the sweep of heavy lashes when she blinked rapidly, the meticulously manicured nails that bit into her forearm.

Rosemary was a delightful mixture of dreamer and modern, independent woman. She was bright, usually cheerful and unrelenting in her quest for success as a commercial designer. She was also totally oblivious to the fact that she was heartstoppingly beautiful. Her vision had always been directed outward.

Ryan could easily call up the memory of the first time they'd met, five years ago at a house party on Long Island....

He was in New York to arrange expansion financing for his carpet-manufacturing business. Rosemary was a young woman, ambitious to a degree almost unknown among the women in the small, Southern town where he'd grown up. She was filled with determination even then, and talented—very, very talented.

From the beginning he was fascinated by her purpose, her will...and her beauty. Though he'd become accustomed to stunning women, the combination of hair, black and heavy as midnight on a moonless night, and eyes the color of sapphires sent him reeling.

She was already firmly established on the first step of the ladder, though still awaiting admission to one of New York's finest graduate schools of design. Right away Ryan recognized that Rosemary would never be content to limit herself to one phase of design, so that the temptation to hire her had never really come to anything. Still, he was enchanted and overcome by his reaction to the lovely young woman.

A long-controlled feeling of bitterness unexpect-

edly swelled at the memory. Automatically he
reached inside his coat to his shirt pocket, until he
remembered he'd quit smoking.

During that interlude he had made a brief attempt at seduction, which had been met with
amused tolerance. The truth was that five years ago
Rosemary Addison had been much too busy to become involved in anything so distracting as an affair. When he offered more she tried to let him
down gently, suggesting friendship in place of romance. Managing to hide the extent of his torment
at her rejection, Ryan accepted her offer.

He had learned to live with his regret, but the
process had been long and painful. He'd focused
totally on his work, thankful that his business, too,
had been demanding in those days.

He set his glass on the table beside his chair and
rose. Concern was *all* he would allow himself to
feel now—concern for the woman he had once
wanted as so much more than a friend. But he
knew he could never want her that way again.
Sighing heavily, he responded to her need, hoping
to lift the burden from her shoulders. As he joined
her at the window the wheels in his mind began to
turn, seeking an answer.

He took her into his arms. It was a gentle embrace, caring and compassionate; they had shared
many of these. He stroked the length of her spine
with one hand while the other massaged the nape
of her neck; the tendons were as tight as a bow
string. This was worse than he had feared. Rosie

had a knack for releasing tension—with a burst of temper if necessary—but whatever was inside this time seemed determined not to release itself. He frowned above her head, knowing a moment of fear for her. She was so independent, and not one to bend. When the release came how destructive would it be?

She spoke into his shirtfront. He had to drop his head to hear the whisper. "It's so good...I needed you, Ryan."

Dear Lord, he thought, *is this Rosie? This meek waif with the uncertain voice?* Where was the feisty devil who was always in control? What had happened to the ambitious woman who had told him five years ago that she didn't need a man to make her happy, she could manage quite well on her own.

"I'm here." His tone was reassuring, but his anxiety increased.

Rosemary lifted her head. "You always have been. I can't tell you how much that means to me."

Feeling his heart throb out of tempo, Ryan almost gave in to the temptation to drown in those beautiful eyes, to taste those beautiful lips. Desire caught him unaware and left him shaken. He hadn't felt this way about Rosemary in years. She was his friend, she had a problem, she needed him, he told himself firmly. A sexual advance would only complicate her life right now. "Hey," he teased unsteadily, "what happened to ambition, success? I seem to remember your saying once that they were more reliable than a man any day."

"They don't seem as important as they once did," she admitted. "I've finally faced the fact that they don't keep you warm on a cold winter's night."

What was she saying? If the words had been spoken by any other woman, they would have immediately signaled a come-on. Rosie probably didn't even know how provocative she sounded. "Don't worry, Rosie. Ambition and success are jealous lovers. They'll be back. I have no doubt on that score," he said heavily, touching her nose with a finger. "Those two have been your companions for too long to simply fade into the background, and a man would have to be crazy to try to compete with them."

"You make me sound rather ruthless, Ryan. And heartless."

He knew what she was feeling. She had a lot of pride, his little Rosie. "And you don't like that, do you?" His sarcasm was cruel, he realized suddenly, wishing the words unsaid. He tempered his tone. "Not ruthless or heartless, sweetheart. Just single-minded."

She pulled out of his embrace and straightened. Her chin came up. At that moment he had never been so proud of her, while at the same time he wondered if he had made an unforgivable mistake. The thought brought him up short. He questioned where on earth it had come from.

A pulse beat in her throat like a tiny bird, fluttering under the skin, anxious to be free. "I'm sorry,

Ryan. I didn't mean to dump my troubles on you like this." She laughed unsteadily. "I sound like one of those frantic women on the prowl that you so despise, don't I?"

He laughed at that. Ryan was aware that Rosemary knew his motto—nothing more serious with a woman than a week in the Caribbean—but they never discussed their relationships with other people. He decided to help her out. "Don't fish, Rosemary," he told her with a teasing lightness he was far from feeling. "I'd never mistake you for one of those where I'm concerned."

His smile was self-mocking. He turned away to rake an impatient hand through his hair, and to shield his expression from her.

Rosemary watched the broad shoulders and forced herself to match his casual tone, but she was horribly embarrassed. "I'm relieved." Wanting to freshen her drink, she picked it up on the way to the bar. "You've always been a good friend, Ryan." She dumped the contents of her glass into the tiny sink. Picking up ice cubes with silver tongs, she started all over.

"And friendship is a lot more dependable than a love affair."

Ryan's comment was exactly what Rosemary needed to pull herself forcibly back from the well of self-pity she'd been dipping into for weeks. "A love affair? Is that what you think I need?" she joked. A sudden, unbidden image flashed through her mind: Ryan as a lover, his gray eyes smoldering like liquid pewter, his sensual mouth... She looked blankly at the decanters. What did she want of him? Finally, with a toss of her head she splashed Scotch over the ice and added water. "Actually, I did consider..." She let her voice trail off, horrified at what she'd been about to reveal.

Ryan followed her. He propped a hip against the counter to watch and sipped from his glass. "Just like that? Rather cold-blooded thinking wasn't it?"

She knew that his unrelenting gaze saw too much. She should explain further. Lord, she was scared. She must have been scared *and* crazy to say what she'd just said to Ryan. At one time he had been attracted to her, and she'd rejected that attraction. The friendship they had managed to salvage had developed into something very precious, unique. The thought of placing that friendship in jeopardy was unbearable.

"I was joking. A poor joke, I'm afraid," she said, quickly taking a sip of the drink to hide her nervousness. "The stereo is in the cabinet by the fireplace. Why don't you put on some albums while I check on dinner?"

There was really nothing to check on. The caterer had left the rack of lamb and accompanying vegetables in her warming oven, along with tiny yeast rolls. The salad and chilled vichyssoise were in the refrigerator, and dessert was a colorful bowl of fresh fruit with assorted cheeses. The only remaining task was to pour the water into the espresso machine, and it wasn't time for that.

Rosemary placed her hands on the counter and leaned heavily on them, trying to relieve some of the tension cramping her shoulders. Not even the death of her father almost a year ago had left her feeling so lost. She'd never particularly needed crowds of people around her, but now she found herself chronically lonely.

Systematically she had begun to alter her lifestyle, hoping the task would jolt her out of the doldrums. Moving into this apartment had been the first step. Antique bric-a-brac lovingly collected by a mother she had never known was packed away. Paintings acquired over the years were crated. Now her father's life surrounded her.

The second step was to plunge headlong into the social whirl of Manhattan. She had had no pressing commissions, and it was a good thing. Every night she had attended a party, the theater or a concert, or accepted a dinner invitation from one of the men ready to escort the talented, well-to-do Rosemary Addison.

She had tried, she really had tried to develop a relationship with one of them. Oh, not an affair—despite her remarks she wasn't that cold-blooded. They were all charming, dynamic, intelligent men, but there was a flaw in each of them. One was too arrogantly self-assured; another, too servile. One only liked Italian food; another was addicted to darkly meaningful theater. Her failure to respond to any of them had added to her frustration. What was wrong with her?

Rosemary was astute enough to realize that delving into a shallow affair could destroy her. She had never been one to indulge in casual sex. She wasn't in love with anyone. Ryan was the only man except for her late father with whom she was totally comfortable, one of the few who had never been intimidated by her success.

Ryan. Unconsciously her eyes sought and found a polished conch shell on the shelf above the coffee maker. When she reached for it, her fingers encountering the cool surface of the delicate peach lip, tender thoughts flooded her memory, taking her back to a summer five years ago....

ROSEMARY'S APPLICATION had been in the files of Design Resources, Inc. for six weeks, the next phase of a career carefully planned from the start. When she had first begun to show an interest in design art, her father had been delighted; but his warning still rang in her ears. "If you're going to be a designer, be the best damn designer in New York City. You should never settle for less. Establishing yourself in a successful career is important for a woman now, but this is a strongly competitive field. If you don't have the ambition to go to the top, don't make the attempt. If you do, a marriage and family will have to wait."

She had the talent, there was no doubt about that. Her father had instilled the drive and ambition, but the talent was all hers. Two years' full-time experience in a small design company after college had equipped her with a portfolio for presentation to the best firm in New York.

The waiting was an insidious form of torture. She hadn't been sleeping well, her appetite had disappeared, and she'd been living on her nerves for six weeks. When her father insisted that she accept the invitation to visit their friends the Shaws on Long Island for a week or two of rest, she protested. "What if DRI should call?"

Her father soothed her qualms. "I promise to get in touch with you immediately."

She didn't want to go to the shore. This job was the most important thing in the world to her, and she wanted only to sit by the telephone; however, she realized her attitude was self-defeating. Reluctantly she agreed to visit Adele and Lawrence Shaw.

HER FATHER'S CHAUFFEUR was unloading her luggage when Adele came down the steps of the beach house to greet her. "Rosemary! I'm so glad you're here with us. Your father says you needed a change." The vivacious redhead leaned closer to whisper, "I think we have just the prescription for you."

When Rosemary stepped into the cool oasis of the living room, she was afraid she knew what Adele meant. By the time her eyes had adjusted from the bright sunlight, she was sure of it.

Adele loved to pair people off. It was a hobby of hers, and the sight of the man who rose to his feet at her entrance immediately put Rosemary on her guard.

"Rosemary, I'd like to present Ryan Tarleton from Georgia. He's in carpet."

Unwittingly Rosemary's lips twitched. She noticed the answering gleam in the handsome man's eyes; neither of them could say a word while Adele rattled on.

"Lawrence predicts Ryan will be his biggest customer someday. He has great faith in this young man." Lawrence was a banker. "Of course I told him Ryan is already his biggest customer." Adele's laughter trilled over their heads.

I see what you mean about big, thought Rosemary as she lifted her eyes to the strong face. Ryan Tarleton must have been six-three or -four and, despite the flush of embarrassment coloring his jaw, evidently self-assured.

He was older than she, probably in his early thirties. White teeth flashed in contrast to a dark, bushy mustache. His smile went straight to her heart, and she melted under the glow. Though she knew what Adele's motives were, and though she fully recognized the trap, Rosemary could no more help walking into it than she could stop breathing.

Admitting silently that this time Adele had outdone herself, Rosemary extended her hand. From the instant he wrapped her fingers in his warm, engulfing grasp, sending tentacles of anticipation up her arm, she knew this man was going to be something special in her life.

2

THE DAYS AT THE SHORE were enchanted. Ryan and Rosemary walked on the beach under the full moon. They searched out quaint places to eat, the quietest places with the dimmest lighting so they could lose themselves in each other. Their dreams and ambitions were shared openly without a thought for the fact that they had just met. The time of discovery was so very limited that they talked nonstop for three days before they even kissed.

That first kiss...she would never forget it. If she had thought about it, she probably would have expected it to happen in some romantic spot, beside the sea bathed in moonlight, or perhaps at the small club where they had danced, on the front-porch swing or under the grape arbor. With romance all around them, she would have expected it to happen anywhere except the laundry room.

At the Shaws' beach house, guests took care of themselves. There was a full-time cook and a maid who came once a week, but everyone pitched in when it came to sandy towels and wet bathing suits. Adele and Lawrence had gone into the city for the day. They had dismissed the cook, telling her they would eat at a favorite seafood spot in the village that night.

Rosemary and Ryan, after an afternoon of swimming and sunning, separated at the top of the stairs to shower. They met again on the way down, carrying wet towels and suits. He grinned and teased her about her red cheeks. "The permanent blush matches your shorts, but you'll probably peel tomorrow."

Ryan wore faded jeans that clung to his lean hips. Rosemary made a face at him, thinking nevertheless that he looked like a picture of what the perfect man should be, with his broad shoulders and chest matted with dark hair.

Before preceding her down the steps he dumped his wet things into her arms and shrugged into a clean white shirt, not bothering to button it. "A pity about your burn, but then I'm partial to broiled lobster," he added.

"You have enough salt in your mustache to season several lobsters," she retorted.

He paused at the bottom of the stairs. There was a decorative shell-rimmed mirror there, and he leaned forward to check, smoothing the brush on his upper lip with a thumb and forefinger. She sailed past him to the back hallway.

"How do you know that's salt?" he asked, catching up with her at the door to the laundry room. "You haven't tasted it." Her back was to him. "Do you realize, Ms Addison, that we've never kissed?" he added, his voice suddenly low.

Though her heart had begun to pound heavily at his words, Rosemary tossed a smile over her shoulder. She closed the door to the dryer and pushed the button to start the action. Then she turned to face him, the smile still playing across her lips. "Of course I realize it. We haven't stopped talking long enough."

He caught his breath, taking a step toward her at the same time she turned. "Rosie...?" His hands came up to lightly grip her shoulders.

No one had ever called her Rosie, but in Ryan's deep, husky voice the nickname sounded wonderful. She swayed slightly at the sensation provoked by the aura of him—clean, sunwashed and totally male. Her lips parted expectantly; she lifted her hands to his bare chest. The crisp, wiry hair tickled her palms, and the warmth of the tanned skin beneath seemed to invite her fingers to explore.

Suddenly his arms came around to catch her close. The well-formed mouth opened over hers.... She felt that first kiss all the way to her toes, curling them against the tiled floor. At twenty-four Rosemary was not innocent, but she had never felt the rightness, the sensation of having come home, that she felt in Ryan's embrace.

In the beginning his lips were knowing but gentle, exploring the pliant shape of hers. As the kiss deepened, though, his mouth grew hungrier for more, and when he felt her willing response, when her tongue joined his in a probing of its own, his control seemed to snap.

His breath, the wonderful breath of his life, filled her mouth as he whispered her name over and over. Rosemary wiggled her arms free to wrap them around his neck. Their bodies met length to length at last; she almost cried out at the thrill of contact. He was so warm, so strong. Somehow he had switched their positions so that he was leaning against the dryer and she was drawn between his thighs into the cradle of his hips.

Her eyes, barely slits, drifted completely shut. Her breasts swelled against the confinement of her bra, and she sighed in relief when he slid his hands under her knit shirt to release the hook.

Ryan lifted his head for a moment. Rosemary forced her heavy lids open, not understanding why she'd lost the wonderful, persuasive pressure of his lips. "Ryan...?"

"I want to see your face when I touch you," he murmured huskily. He moved his hands across her back and around to cup her breasts. She heard his breath catch in unison with hers. Their eyes held. It was a moment that seemed to stretch forever, but was over too soon.

Caution bells went off in her mind. *This can't be happening,* she thought, *not to me. Not now!* From the first she had known Ryan was more important to her than other men she knew, but she hadn't realized how important.

She must have made some negative movement, for suddenly his hands left her breasts and came up to frame her face, his fingers sliding into her wet hair. His thumbs made soothing motions on her cheeks. The silver eyes roamed over her features with a loving, reassuring tenderness. "You are bewitching." His voice was unsteady, his smile tremulous. "I've only known you three days, and I'm totally infatuated with you."

Fighting for sanity, she brought her arms down to wedge between their bodies. "I know," she whispered. "It seems like longer."

"I would never hurt you, Rosie." His expression was very serious, and she smiled.

"Do you think I don't know that, Ryan?"

"Then what did I see in your eyes?"

She sighed, snaking her arms around his torso, resting her cheek against his chest, holding him and hiding from him.

But Ryan was perceptive. He tilted her face up with one broad hand, searching her eyes until she thought he had read all the way to her soul. "What?" he repeated.

She could be nothing but candid. "Regret. This is too strong, too quick, and I'm not ready for it. It frightens me. I can't handle an affair, Ryan."

"What if I had something more permanent in mind?"

"So soon? That would be worse," she said honestly. "We hardly know each other."

Slowly Ryan studied each feature as though memorizing her eyes, her lips, her nose and forehead, her chin. Finally he released her. "Okay. It's all right. I understand."

Do you, she wondered. *Do you really?*

THE MOOD of the remaining days was frantic with gaiety while shadowed by poignancy. Rosemary was torn. She wanted to be with Ryan as much as possible before their time had to end.

He was a man who touched as easily as he laughed, and each affectionate touch was a beautiful memory to be stored in her heart. Memories would have to do, because there was a world out there she had sworn to conquer. She wasn't ready for an affair, or marriage, or any kind of committed relationship.

When her father called to inform her that she had been accepted by DRI, it was almost an anticlimax. She faced saying goodbye to Ryan with anticipation and dread. The last day she found tears welling in her eyes at the slightest provocation, but she forced them back. She knew instinctively that he was hurting. She hurt, too. But it couldn't be too serious, could it? This was a summer romance. She would get over it, and so would he.

They walked the moonlit beach one last time, their hands linked loosely, the night before she was to leave. Silence stretched between them like a vast wasteland, arid and barren.

All at once he stopped, pulling her around to face him.

No! Rosemary knew what was coming, and she wanted to cry. *No, Ryan. Don't do this.*

"Rosemary, will you marry me?" he said.

The answer was on her lips even as he asked the question, ready and waiting to be delivered before she had a chance to think what was unthinkable. "I can't."

To her surprise he smiled. The curve of his lips was bittersweet and sad, but it was a smile. He tucked a strand of hair behind her ear. "I knew what you'd say, but I couldn't let you leave without asking."

"Ryan, I'm sorry."

"Honey, don't." He choked slightly on the words, lifting his gaze to look long over the calm sea. The moonlight etched his profile in silver. When he spoke again his voice was steady. "It could have been so fine between us. But the timing is wrong, I can see that."

"I have something to ask of you, too." Her eyes were shiny with moisture.

"Anything." He caught one bright, unshed tear on a fingertip. "You know that."

"I care about you, Ryan," she said, wincing as his hand tightened involuntarily on her fingers. "You must know you're special to me, and I don't want to—to lose touch. Will you still be my friend?"

Wrapping her in a hard embrace, he whispered, "Yes. Yes, Rosie. I'll always be your friend."

She didn't see him again for a year.

"ARE YOU GOING TO SPEND the evening in the kitchen?" Ryan's voice startled her out of her reverie.

She turned to smile at him, arrested for a moment between the past and the present. He was standing in the open doorway with an arm on each side of the jamb. He almost filled the space. The sight of his large, well-proportioned body left her as breathless as his first kiss in the laundry room had. Her eyes dropped involuntarily to his mouth. Five years...

He lifted an enquiring brow. "Rosie?"

With a nervous twist she whirled from the gaze that always saw too much. "Everything's ready. I hope you're hungry."

He grinned. "Don't try to con me into believing you cooked."

Glancing over her shoulder, she relaxed at the teasing light in his eyes and returned the grin. "Why should I cook when there's a perfectly good caterer next door?"

"It doesn't look to me like he's been feeding you very well. How much weight have you lost?"

"Not much."

"C'mon, Rosie," he chided in a tone as dry as dust. "I know you hate the kitchen. How often do you bother to have meals brought in?"

She should have responded to the light reprimand as it had been offered, with a teasing answer. Teasing seemed beyond her for some reason. "Certainly not every night. Honestly, Ryan, I may not *like* to cook, but I can certainly prepare a meal," she told him crossly.

He persisted. "A meal? As in peanut-butter sandwich?"

They both knew her weakness for peanut butter in any form—in cookies, spread on bananas and rolled in nuts, or straight from a spoon—she adored it. Finally she relented. "Peanut butter is very nourishing," she informed him cheerfully. "Here." She handed him a bottle of wine and a corkscrew. "Make yourself useful."

Later as they lingered over espresso, she caught Ryan studying her with a searching look.

"I can't stand to see you doing this to yourself, you know," he stated flatly. "I do care about you."

"Doing what?" She tried for indifference, her eyes focused on the stark arrangement of grayed-green orchids in the center of the table, and ignored the last half of his statement. She had managed to keep the conversation on an easy level during dinner; now she felt the knot in her stomach that warned her of returning tension.

"Dammit, Rosie!" Ryan pushed his cup away and leaned forward, crossing his arms on the table. His eyes caught and held hers.

"Ryan, I know what's happening to me. I'm not dumb."

A dimple flashed in his cheek as he smiled. "No, sweetheart, you're not dumb. So tell me. What's happening?"

"I'm having a panic reaction to the prospect of my thirtieth birthday. And maybe a bit of burnout, as well. That's all it is. I'll get over it," she said, but she wondered. Was that the extent of her problem?

Or was she just trying to excuse herself to Ryan, to quiet his speculation?

"Well, if that's all..." He chuckled. "You'll survive your thirtieth birthday. I guarantee it. Several of us have, you know."

"You devil." Rosemary gave him a jab. She picked up a spoon to stir her coffee, a useless move, since it was black. "I'm sure that's all it is," she said again.

"Then I have a proposition for you."

She lifted a delicately arched brow, grateful that he, at least, couldn't hear the pulse that threatened to drown out all sound from her ears.

He laughed. "Not that kind of proposition."

The brow went higher. Her gaze was caught in the silvery depths of his for a minute before she could wrench away. "What is your proposition?" She was long past the age of blushing, but her face felt hot.

"I'm in New York this trip to look for a carpet designer for a new line. I want you to take the job."

Rosemary stared at him. She was oddly let down and angry with herself for feeling that way. What had she expected? If Ryan had picked up the rather obvious gauntlet she'd thrown down before dinner, she would have backed off, wouldn't she? "I've never designed carpeting before. I don't know anything about it." But she propped her chin on her hand, diverted and ready to listen.

"Carpet design isn't very different from any other. If you can't handle the mechanics, we'll get someone else to transfer your ideas into working designs.''

Cocking her head to one side, she tapped her cheek with a rosy-tipped nail. It was an interesting idea. She did a lot of graphic work in offices, had even done wallpaper designs. To be able to coordinate the entire look with the addition of a proper floor covering was tempting. Rosemary grinned at him, feeling better. ''Why me?'' she asked, looping a swathe of black hair behind her ear.

Ryan relaxed. ''You're fishing again, honey. You know you're the best. From the time you were twenty-two and designing T-shirts, you've been the best.''

She didn't bother to demur. Maybe she wasn't the best, but she was damn close. She was ''Rosemary,'' tops in her field in a city where being tops counted for something.

Only in the past few months had she begun to speculate that in stressing career success, she might have robbed herself of the common pleasures of being a woman. True, no scenes, tears, recriminations or jealousy marred her life, but neither had there been room for intimacy, softness or sentiment. She was everything she—and her father—had expected her to be.

Ryan was watching expressions flit across her face, and he might have been reading her mind when he spoke again. ''Even your father would be pleased,'' he told her wryly. ''We're starting a new premium line for offices and commercial buildings.

It's a risky proposition at this point, but I think your designs would be a strong selling point. We'll name the line 'Rosemary,' of course.''

Rosemary was surprised at that. She knew Ryan's carpet lines were traditionally named for cities—Newport, Savannah, St. Louis.

''I've just shelled out several million for a new German tufting machine which, according to the manufacturer, will do everything but roast a turkey. The possibilities for design are almost limitless,'' he added, sweetening the bait.

''Hmm. It might really be interesting.'' She felt her enthusiasm grow. A new challenge, she thought, throwing off the pall of depression for the first time in months.

''Besides, it would get you out of New York for a while, and that's what you need right now.''

That was unexpected. Her head jerked around, fanning the black cloud of her hair across her shoulders. ''What do you mean? I can design from here.''

Ryan shook his head decisively. ''No way. I need you on site in case problems crop up. Don't worry. We have superior facilities and a beautiful studio.''

Rosemary didn't doubt that. She was probably one of the few people who knew how the business had been built, brick by brick, out of the efforts of this one man. He had started with a college scholarship and a knowledge of carpet manufacturing gained from summer jobs. When the opportunity to study had come, however, he had chosen to take his major in business rather than textile engineering, and the decision had paid off. He could afford to hire top-notch engineers and designers.

"But, Ryan," she protested, feeling the pressure closing in on her. "I can't leave New York!"

"Why not?" Candlelight failed to soften the harsh planes of his face.

"Well...I..." She looked across the polished floor to her living room.

When Ryan spoke again she was shocked by the impatience in his voice. "Why not?" he repeated. "Because the ice queen has finally moved herself into an ice palace, and she prefers to sit here and freeze to death?"

"No," she choked. Was that what she had done? "No, I don't want to do that."

"I don't believe you. Look around, my dear Rosie." He indicated the entire apartment with a broad sweep of his arm. "Your other place was warm and welcoming. The beautiful antiques might have been heavy with the weight of tradition, but that was a home, not a showroom. There is nothing soft or feminine in this whole damn place. With the exception of the man-eating sofa, every surface reflects a hard image right back at you. Is that what you want? To be constantly confronted with cold images? Do you really like it?" he demanded.

The silence with which she greeted his question was thick with regret. She shook her head. "It's me, after all, Ryan. Isn't it?"

"The hell it is," he grated. "It's you as you picture yourself to be! But this *isn't* you. And you aren't happy with it, Rosie. You've said as much.''

"No, I'm not happy," she admitted at last, tilting her head in an attempt to tease. "Are you trying to save me from myself?''

"Maybe," he said with the first sign of real anger. He had been annoyed, irritated, but not really angry until now. He surged to his feet, his thrust against the chair threatening to overturn it.

Rosemary watched, eyes wide. He paced a few steps and then turned back. "Rosie, your father encouraged you to be a super-achiever— I'm not saying that's bad," he hastened to add when she opened her mouth to defend her father. "But you've never had time to 'stop and smell the roses,' as the song says. Come to Georgia with me, honey," he urged roughly. "Let the Southern sun warm your bones—for a couple of months. This—" he seemed at a loss as he threw a gesture at her living room "—this will all be waiting for you when you get back.''

Maybe. Maybe she could leave the metropolitan environment, the only life she'd known for thirty years to move to a rural setting. Apple Valley wasn't very large, she knew. It would be as alien to her as another country, but maybe a complete change *was* a good idea. "I couldn't come for a while," she said hesitantly, not realizing she had already made the decision.

There was a flash of triumph in Ryan's eyes when he sat down again. "Who knows?" he told her brashly. "You may find you like small-town living."

Obviously he thought he'd scored a victory, and that annoyed her. "Just how small is Apple Valley?"

The smug look disappeared. "Four hundred."

"People?" Rosemary squeaked. Her revenge forgotten, she swallowed over a sudden dryness in her throat. There were more than four hundred people in this block!

"Sanderson is only six miles away."

She was almost afraid to ask. "How large is Sanderson?"

"Five or six thousand," he said nonchalantly.

Rosemary glared at him. "Ryan Tarleton, are you laughing?"

He released the deep chuckle. "Yes, I am. We aren't exactly cut off from civilization, Rosie. Atlanta is only an hour away, close enough for dinner or the theater."

"I'll think about it." She was careful not to let her relief show.

"Why don't I have my New York office draw up a contract for you to consider? Tomorrow night we'll have dinner. You can read it over and ask me whatever you like."

"All right. I'll look at a contract—but I'm not promising anything."

"Of course not." He leaned back in his chair and reached for his cup with a satisfied smile.

3

ROSEMARY TOOK THE PROFFERED HAND and jumped lightly to the tarmac. "Thanks, Stan," she said, flashing a smile at the ruddy-faced young pilot, and another at the shining, corporate jet. "It was a wonderful flight."

"My pleasure, Miss Addison," he answered with a cocky grin.

She looked around curiously at the small municipal airport, the concrete building, the metal hangars off to one side. A wooden sign swinging slightly from a horizontal bar read "Sanderson."

"Mr. Tarleton is over there, ma'am."

Rosemary swiveled her head to follow the direction he indicated. For a moment she was confused.

The only person in sight was a very large man in jeans who was propped against the fender of a dusty gray Lincoln. A sweat-stained Stetson was pulled low over his brow, and his arms were crossed forbiddingly over his chest. That man didn't look at all like Ryan.

She put up a hand to shield her eyes from the glare of the Georgia sun; her jaw fell in astonishment.

Slowly the man unfolded himself from his slouch. Dazzling white teeth contrasted with the full, dark mustache. The smile and the mustache were the only things familiar about him.

"Ryan?" she murmured. She took one tentative step and stopped.

He dropped his arms. "Hello, Rosie." The deep, vibrant voice and easy gait as he walked forward had a most unusual effect on her. It *was* Ryan. He approached slowly as though to give her plenty of time to adjust to the change.

Rosemary shook her head slightly to negate the feeling of being in a dream. Nothing was as it should be. Where were the hand-tailored suits and silk shirts? Where was the sophisticated, urbane man she was accustomed to seeing in elegant dinner clothes?

The individual who stood before her in that attractive, lazy stance was earthy, dynamic and very, very male. She actually gulped in amazement.

The sleeves of his blue work shirt were rolled to his elbows, three of the front buttons unfastened. The exposed skin was tanned to a golden brown and shaded further by a lavish sprinkling of dark, curling hair.

It had been so very long since she'd seen him in any but the the most formal situations. She had almost forgotten this sensual Ryan. Seeing him like this brought the memories back in a rush.

"Welcome South, sweetheart." His words interrupted her thoughts, but not the strange furious rate of her pulse.

Rosemary was oblivious to the fresh smell of spring in the air, at such variance with the cold caverns of New York City that she had left behind. She didn't see beyond the airstrip to the rolling hills strewn with flowering dogwood trees, or to the grinning face of the pilot as he stowed her luggage in the trunk of the Lincoln and handed Ryan a briefcase. She was completely hypnotized by the sight of the man before her—Ryan Tarleton as she had known him for five years, yet a Ryan she had never known at all. For this certainly was not the rather appealing and much younger Ryan of five years ago.

He was so different that she almost put out her hand to touch him, to see if he was real. This man, though every inch as attractive as the Ryan she knew so well, was seasoned by another kind of experience, and the realization intimidated Rosemary slightly. At least she thought what she felt was intimidation. He provoked some kind of very strong feeling, anyway.

Ryan shook the young pilot's hand and thanked him. Rosemary added her own thanks again, but vaguely, without taking her eyes from Ryan's face.

Only last month she had seen him, dearly familiar, in her Manhattan apartment. This might be another man in another lifetime, or a man from a lifetime years past with whom she was renewing acquaintance. The experience was disconcerting but exciting. After all, wasn't this what she had wanted? When she'd agreed to come here, she must have been hoping, subconsciously, for a change from the limited relationship she and Ryan had shared for the past five years.

Mentally she scolded herself. That wasn't the reason at all. She had come to design a line of carpet, and...to...well, for a number of reasons. But when Ryan helped her into the car with a hand at her elbow, the searing sensation there warned her it wasn't going to be easy to keep her mind on business in the face of his increased magnetism.

He tossed his briefcase onto the back seat. "You'll be staying in a small cottage not far from the plant. It's furnished, but if you'd feel more comfortable with your own things, we'll pay moving expenses, of course."

The two-lane road curled around the edge of a shopping center. A supermarket, movie theater and drugstore dominated the area, with various other smaller shops tucked in between.

Rosemary took all this in before finally allowing her gaze to swing to Ryan, then immediately regretted the move. She couldn't look away. In the work shirt his shoulders appeared twice as broad. The jeans molded his muscular thighs in a potent fit that a Brooks Brothers suit could never hope to rival. He'd tossed the Stetson into the back seat, and his dark-brown hair was rumpled. She made a fist to keep her fingers from reaching up to smooth it away from his forehead. He was speaking, but the words went right over her head.

"Rosie?"

One smoldering glance from those smoky gray eyes and her hands began to tremble, her voice died in her throat, and the dull thud of the pulse in her temple sounded in her ears like a base drum. So that was what was wrong with her. Dear heaven, she was attracted to Ryan. More than attracted, she was mesmerized.

He finally raised an inquiring brow, and the dimple in his cheek deepened. "Will I pass?" he asked.

"Huh?"

"I said," he explained patiently, "we'll move your things down if you want them. I have trucks going to New York three times a week, or we'll pay for a regular moving company."

"Oh. Well. Why don't I wait…uh…" Dear Lord! She had to get hold of herself. She was acting like a fluttery hen. "We'll s-see," she finished weakly and subsided against the seat.

Ryan tactfully ignored her stammering. "You're now in downtown Sanderson," he told her after a minute.

Rosemary looked out the side window, grateful for an excuse to shift her attention from the man next to her. "What a charming town." The Georgian front of a contemporary building dominated the intersection of two roads. "Wellman County Court House," she read out loud. Stores of all kinds spread out from the hub. Their facades were freshly painted, and large pots of geraniums stood at the doors of one or two of them.

As they drove a block farther she was surprised to see houses. "You mean that's all there is of it?" she asked weakly.

Ryan laughed, a rich, hearty sound. She thought with fleeting pleasure that she'd never heard him laugh that way in New York.

"There are shopping centers and restaurants, but not in the center of town," he told her with a grin.

She was watching his hands when he flicked on his turn signal and maneuvered the car into the left lane. Hazily she wondered why the small shaft didn't snap off in the face of such strength. Then, with a jolt, she remembered the touch of his hands, clearly and precisely. But hers were not thoughts of the touch of a friend. She remembered, as though the years had been obliterated, the gentle caresses of a man who might have been a lover had the circumstances been different. "How am I supposed to get to these places?" she asked hastily in an attempt to divert her thoughts.

When the turn was complete he said, "I've arranged a car for you—an EXP with a sun roof. It's red." He shot his grin at her again. "It won't be delivered until tomorrow, though."

"On Sunday?" Her voice was husky and slightly choked.

"You'll find that small-town people are accommodating. I've had someone stock your cottage with a few basic groceries, but tonight we're going out to a barbecue restaurant for dinner. You have to sample hickory-smoked barbecue on your first night in Georgia.''

Rosemary had become very quiet at this speech; when she didn't answer he glanced over. Annoyance clipped his voice. ''It isn't pheasant, Rosie, but it's very good,'' he said defensively.

''It isn't that, Ryan.'' Her eyes were focused beyond the windshield, though she didn't see the mountain in front of them.

They had made another turn, and this road wasn't as heavily traveled. Ryan steered the car onto the grassy shoulder, then switched off the ignition with an impatient twist of his wrist. He turned to look at her, his arm resting along the back of the seat. ''Honey, I know it isn't what you're used to, but it will be all right, I promise you.'' A strand of hair had escaped from her chignon; he tucked it behind her ear. ''Give it a chance, Rosie. It's a nice community. The people are friendly. Give it a chance.''

She dropped her chin and mouthed the words, I can't drive, but no sound came out.

''What?'' His fingers curved on her nape, urging her face toward his.

''I said, I can't drive.''

Ryan stared at her, speechless. She fidgeted under his stunned gaze. ''Don't look at me as though I have two heads! Why would I want a car in the city?'' she asked irritably.

''I didn't think about that,'' he said softly, almost to himself.

The fingers at her nape toyed with errant strands of dark, silky hair. She tried unsuccessfully to control the shiver that traveled down her spine.

"Well, you'll just have to learn," he told her more briskly.

A hint of amusement in his eyes that he couldn't hide annoyed her even more than her reaction to his touch. "What if I'm not interested in learning?" she asked defiantly.

Before she realized what was happening, the atmosphere in the car changed as suddenly as though a bolt of lightning had charged the air. Ryan put an arm around her shoulders to haul her across the seat. His eyes were riveted on her mouth, his expression almost curious. His other hand tangled in her sleek hair, threatening the chignon further as his head descended slowly but unfalteringly.

Surprise parted her lips, and he took full advantage. His mouth settled over hers with familiarity, as though they had kissed yesterday, but it had been a long, long time since Ryan had kissed her like this. His tongue swept inside to explore every curve, every surface with disturbing possession.

Rosemary felt herself responding with a helplessness totally alien to her. Tentatively her tongue met his, but instead of deepening the kiss, he chuckled, his warm breath filling her mouth. His lips curved over hers, his mustache brushing, tickling.

With an effort she opened her eyes, to see an unreadable gleam in his. "W-what was that for?"

The resonance in his voice was as unfamiliar as his expression, but there was a certain huskiness there, too. "I've never seen you vulnerable, Rosie. It's rather appealing." His thumb outlined her full lips, and his voice dropped another octave. "It's been a long time between kisses."

She didn't pretend to misunderstand, but her eyes fell beneath his warm gaze. "Yes," she answered simply. "That sort of kiss, anyway. You're so different."

In fascination she watched the expressions that chased across his face. He chose to ask for an explanation, although one wasn't necessary. "What do you mean?"

"I mean here, in your element, you're—"

The interruption, when it came, was delivered in a strange tone, almost harsh. "I'm not different, the setting is. Maybe you just never bothered to get to know the real man, Rosie."

Unable to understand his sudden irritation, she spoke quietly. "That isn't true, Ryan. You must know how surprised I am."

"Yes, I know," he admitted wryly.

She lifted a hand to touch his rough cheek, half expecting him to pull away. He didn't. He sat very still, tolerating her touch, until she sighed and dropped her hand to her lap. "I have a feeling I'll need to be different, too. To tell you the truth, I'm scared to death. I'm going to be like a fish out of water in Apple Valley, U.S.A...." Her eyes met the unspoken agreement in his. "But I'm glad I came," she added softly.

"I'm glad you came, too," he said at last. Leaving a kiss on the tip of her nose, he released her, moving back to his side of the car. The moment of tension was over. He didn't speak again until they were on the road; then he laughed.

If there was strain in the laughter she couldn't tell, but the sound sent goose bumps up her spine. "What's so funny?"

"There are no subways in Apple Valley," he teased, seemingly himself again. "You'll have to learn to drive, and I suppose I'll have to be the one to teach you."

Relaxing, Rosemary reluctantly returned his grin. "Well, if you're going to teach me, it can't be too difficult." At last she was beginning to regain her spunk.

A glimmer of appreciation appeared in his eyes as he glanced over at her. "I had to teach my high-school sweetheart to drive, and it was a disaster," he warned. "I ended up almost wringing her neck. Who knows—maybe I've mellowed since then."

"I hope so. I don't relish having my neck wrung."

The rest of the short ride passed in silence. Rosemary was lost in her thoughts. The kiss had released all kinds of memory snatches, all the feelings and emotions that had been firmly squelched five years ago. But they had not died, oh, no. They had only lain dormant, waiting for a time, a place, to spring to life again. She felt the stirrings of a need she hadn't dreamed she would ever feel, ever want. She wondered if that realization—for he couldn't have failed to notice her response to the kiss—was what had sparked Ryan's brief resentment.

When he finally turned into a graveled driveway Rosemary straightened in her seat. The drive curved in front of a small white cottage nestled in the shadow of a tree-covered mountain as though it had always belonged there. She had to lean forward to see the top of the peak. "What a beautiful spot!"

Ryan smiled and took her hand. Opening his door, he tugged her across the seat and out on his side. "Leave your things. I want to show you around."

The silence was the first thing she noticed. Initially she thought it to be absolute, but then the whisper of a breeze rustling new leaves reached her ears, and a bird sang a light, sweet song. She heard the annoyed chatter of a small animal and looked around for the source. "Is that the country mouse?" She laughed, but warily, pointing to the front doorstep, where a tiny creature no more than four inches tall sat frowning at them.

Ryan laughed. A thumb tilted the Stetson farther back on his head. "That's a chipmunk, but I guess a country mouse would be more appropriate."

And I'm the city mouse, thought Rosemary. *Will I be so out of place that I'll turn tail and run for home like the small creature in the children's story?* She shook off those morose feelings and brought her attention back to her surroundings.

A split-rail fence cornered one section of the lawn. Yellow roses spilled in colorful confusion over the rough, unpainted barrier. She stooped to touch a blossom, which nodded, releasing its fragrance. The scent was sweet and fresh.

"Flowers," she breathed. "Real flowers, growing from the ground. Oh, Ryan, I'm going to love this!"

He drew her in under his arm and murmured distractedly as he searched her features, "I hope so, Rosie. I hope I haven't..."

His arm was heavy on her shoulders, but it wasn't an unwelcome heaviness. It warmed her through with a sensation of security. "Haven't what?" she asked after a moment when he didn't continue.

"Haven't put both of us in a tenuous position. Come on. I have something I want to show you before we go inside." His arm still circling her shoulders, he guided her around to the back of the house.

At the sight that greeted her, Rosemary caught her breath and moved away from his arm like a sleepwalker. Never—never had she seen anything like this in her life. She walked forward with the illusion of having stepped into a painting, or into an illustration from a child's picture book.

The back of the house overlooked a shaded ravine at the foot of the mountain. Dappled sunlight played in the sparkling water of a small stream below. A willow tree, weeping and bent with age, trailed its branches in the water. The sloped ground was carpeted with brown needles from towering pines, while hundreds of white, flowering dogwood trees formed clouds beneath the canopy of green. Wild flowers grew in profusion, punctuating the enchanting scene with color.

Rosemary turned, her excitement reflected in her eyes, to find Ryan studying her.

He stood with his feet planted wide apart, his hands resting lightly on his hips, a giant of a man. His shield of sophistication was completely gone now, exposing the nature of the human being beneath it—totally at home in his environment, sharing this part of his world with her.

Her heart warmed like a glowing hearth on a winter night. "Thank you, Ryan, for bringing me here," she said with deep affection. "I know you were right. This is just what I need." She moved toward him in a rush of gratitude, intending to wind her arms around his waist; but he forstalled her, gripping her upper arms to hold her away.

His expression had altered subtly at her words. He was reserved again but no less considerate. She wondered at the change. "You'd better not thank me yet," he said casually as he turned her toward the house. "You still have to learn to drive. Let's go inside." With one hand at the small of her back, he steered her in the direction of the back door, fishing a key out of the pocket of his jeans.

The cottage was built "shotgun" style, with a

wide hall from the front door to the back. It was furnished with Early American simplicity and warmth. The shiny hardwood floors were covered with colorful braided rugs, and the few upholstered pieces, added for comfort, were unobtrusive in natural homespun.

The thought occurred to her that perhaps Ryan was trying to make a point of the contrast between her apartment and this charming cottage. If that was true he had succeeded.

There was a homey, hospitable atmosphere here, and she had studied art for long enough to appreciate the beauty of the furnishings. These were not the French and English antiques she was familiar with from her childhood, though the soft patina of oak and maple had been well rubbed through heaven only knew how many generations. These pieces spoke of a pioneer people, struggling to carve some degree of civilization out of a wilderness, and unless she was very much mistaken, some of them were priceless.

As Ryan led the way from room to room her conviction grew that this was no ordinary rental property. This was a house that was lived in and loved.

Her suspicions were confirmed when they stepped into the last bedroom, the one Ryan indicated would be hers. A curved tester bed with a hand-crocheted coverlet dominated the room. A three-legged chair in one corner held a fat cushion of embroidered crewel, the colors rich and beautifully wrought. A blanket chest stood at the foot of the bed, while another taller piece with a mirror set in a simple frame served as a dresser. There was also a slant-front bureau desk with a cane-bottomed chair.

"Ryan, this isn't a cottage. It's a museum! Who would rent out a home like this?"

He grinned ruefully. "You noticed."

"I *am* an art major. Will you please explain?"

He lifted a hand to the door facing and stroked the dark wood, his caress almost loving. "The owner is away."

"Ryan!"

"Okay," he conceded, looking at her again. "This is the old Tarleton home."

"You grew up here?"

"Yes. Though the house hardly looked like this then."

Rosemary knew Ryan's father had died when he was a child, and that his family had had a struggle, but not much more. In the years she'd known him, he seldom talked about his family. She remembered asking once, but when he told her she wouldn't be interested, she had let the subject drop. With a sudden feeling of self-reproach she realized Ryan was right about one thing: she hadn't taken the time to get to know the real man.

"My mother felt that despite the hard times we went through, this should stay with the Tarletons. So I bought it back for her. She had a ball redoing and shopping for the pieces she'd always imagined belonged here. She still lives here, but I have a house on the adjoining property, around that curve." He waved toward the road, visible outside the window.

"Where is your mother now?"

"Visiting my sister, Beth, in England. Beth's husband manages one of my plants there."

"But when will she be back? Won't she mind a stranger living in her home?"

"She'll be gone for at least three months." He grinned. "Beth is expecting a baby at any time, and if I know mother she'll stay with her first grandchild until they kick her out. If you don't want to stay here we'll find you something else, although rental property in Apple Valley is almost nonexistant."

"She won't mind?" Rosemary repeated.

"She knows you're here," Ryan assured her.

"Then I'd love to stay. It's a beautiful house." She smiled, musing for a minute. "It will be interesting, sleeping in the house where you grew up."

Her expression was playful; his was calm. "If you'd like to freshen up I'll bring in your luggage. The bath's through that door."

"Thanks." She shut the door behind her, resting against it for a moment. She looked thoughtfully at the reflection of the woman who stared back at her. It was going to take some time to adjust, both to the changes in Ryan and to living here, but that woman looked fairly optimistic. Turning on the taps, she leaned down to vigorously splash cold water on her face.

If she was alert and observant she might get to know this small-town Ryan better, and she suddenly discovered she wanted that—very, very much.

Ryan had deposited her bags in the bedroom. "I'll leave you to unpack, Rosie, and come back for you about six," he told her when she joined him there.

"All right." One part of her wanted to be by herself to examine her surprising response to him, but the other part was slightly hesitant at being left alone in such an isolated spot. Though she tried to conceal it, the latter reaction must have shown on her face.

"What are you afraid of, sweetheart?" He came closer. She could feel the warmth of his body, smell the tempting masculine scents of soap and outdoors. The spicy after-shave he wore when he was in the city was conspicuously absent.

She smiled up at him, her lips curved doubtfully. "Do you realize this is the first time in my life I've ever been completely alone in a house...a building of any kind?" she asked.

His expression of blank surprise was exactly the same one he'd worn when she told him she couldn't drive. She bit off a laugh. Poor Ryan. He really hadn't thought this all out.

His big hands came up to frame her face, and he looked deeply into her eyes. His voice was surprisingly taut with feeling. "I really have taken you out of your element, haven't I, Rosie? I'm so accustomed to small-town life that I'm afraid I didn't realize..."

His minty breath added another scent to muddle her senses. She made an effort to lighten the atmosphere. "Don't worry about it, Ryan. I'm sure I'll survive. In fact, I'm looking forward to the experience."

WHAT DO *I* WEAR TO THIS BARBECUE RESTAURANT, wondered Rosemary as she stood in front of the closet surveying the clothes she'd just unpacked. The little silk dresses were definitely out, as were the tailored skirts and jackets she'd brought along for office wear and professional meetings. She hadn't owned jeans since she'd decided on her twenty-third birthday that wearing them made her look too young.

With a sniff of disgust at her own hesitation, she pulled a pair of cranberry slacks off a hanger and tossed them across the bed. She retrieved a matching cotton sweater from one dresser drawer and gossamer pink panties and bra from another.

The inclination to waver and vacillate was totally unlike her. What difference did it make what she wore? She quickly stripped out of her traveling clothes and walked naked to the bathroom. She had left the bustle of Manhattan and the contemporary setting of her apartment only a few hours ago, but she felt as though she had stepped into a time machine and been catapulted backward into another century.

The bathroom extended that time-warp sensation. Rosemary hadn't taken a moment to study it before, but now her respect for the unknown woman's flair grew; Ryan's mother hadn't skimped on the remodeling in here. The fixtures were definitely modern, but she had retained the old-worldliness in a clever way.

The glory of a bygone age was reflected in a cheval-glass mirror with a hand-carved frame and brass horizontal pivots. Shining oak floors were protected from splashes by small, brightly colored bath rugs that would be easy to launder. The room was situated in a corner of the house, and the colors in the rugs were startlingly repeated in beautiful stained-glass shutters over the wide windows of two walls.

The designer in Rosemary was impressed by the workmanship of the glass. In the late-afternoon light the vivid turquoise, violet and gold of the floral design held a rich glow; with the morning sunshine pouring through, the colors would be lighter, more cheerful. The gold would turn to buttercup yellow, the violet to heather.

A huge tub, obviously custom-made, sat on claw feet in the center of the large room. Steam rose almost instantly once she turned on the taps. She adjusted the temperature with cold water, then added bath salts from the plentiful supply on one shelf of an antique baker's rack. Another shelf held pots of African violets in bloom, their colors running the gamut from palest pink to deepest purple. The towels stacked on the bottom of the rack vibrantly echoed those colors.

Rosemary stepped into the tub and slid gratefully into the fragrant water. Resting her head against the rim, she closed her eyes.

Ryan immediately sneaked into her thoughts. She tried to envision the sophisticated Ryan, who could, by his mere demeanor, command the best table at any restaurant in New York and who could have three taxis pull over to the curb on Fifth Avenue by lifting one finger, all vying for his trade. That was no mean feat!

The mental picture of that man, however, was blurred by the image of the one in dusty boots, whose virile good looks caused her pulse to accelerate drastically, her breath to catch in her throat. She wasn't a teenager, for heaven's sake; she was a mature woman approaching her thirtieth birthday. Yet she felt she was on the brink of a cliff-hanger relationship, ready—almost sickeningly willing— to plunge headfirst into whatever risk was involved.

She lifted a wet hand to touch her lips. His mouth had been firm and sure over hers. The kiss had been brief but quite thorough. She wondered how it would have felt had he kissed her longer, harder—with hunger for more than a kiss. How it would feel to be pressed against his body, to have his arms wrap around her, his hands move restlessly over her back, his arousal...

Rosemary sat up suddenly, the movement producing a wave that threatened to overflow the tub. Dear Lord, what was she thinking? She was here for a limited period of time. When her job was over she would return to New York and take up her life there, a life that had always been satisfying and complete. She would merge into the anonymity of the city and be once again the independent and capable Rosemary Addison.

Why, then, did the prospect seem so bleak? And why in the hell was she feeling sorry for herself?

WHILE DRESSING, Rosemary forced her self-pity away with deliberation and determination. Of course, to do so she had to force all other introspection away, as well. She avoided a direct look into her own eyes as she applied her makeup for fear of what she might see there.

When Ryan arrived an hour later she was composed enough to greet him nonchalantly. "Hi, Ryan."

His white teeth flashed, and she turned away quickly to pick up her purse from a chair. "I'm ready," she added unnecessarily, joining him at the door.

But he didn't move aside. "You look lovely, Rosie." He stepped across the threshold and leaned down to kiss her lightly on the cheek. His lips lingered there while he inhaled the scent of violets. "Hmm. You smell good, too," he added huskily as his mouth edged closer to hers. "I recognize the fragrance, but somehow it smells different on my mother." He played across her lips with tiny, nipping bites.

The warmth of his breath in her mouth and his own scent of soap and after-shave effectively wiped out all her good resolutions. When he lifted his head she stood there, looking up at him dazedly. "Ryan," she whispered, "you just have to stop doing this."

"Stop doing what, sweetheart?" he asked innocently.

She shook her head to clear it. "Stop kissing me like this—stop with the deep, sexy feeling in your voice." She was pleased to note that her own voice became stronger with each phrase. With a great effort she took a step away from him to appraise his clothes. "Stop looking like the original macho man."

His lips compressed in an effort to cover his amusement. The jeans and pale-blue shirt were clean and pressed, and the boots had evidently enjoyed a swipe with a polishing cloth, but except for those concessions he was the same specimen of masculinity who had met her at the airport. "Rosie, take my word for it. A three-piece suit would be out of place at Barbecue Heaven on Saturday night."

Doubt furrowed her brow. "What about me?" Her clothes were casual, but she wondered if they were casual enough. "Will I fit in?"

Taking her hand in his warm grasp, he pulled her through the door and closed it behind them. "You'll fit in perfectly. As long as you keep your mouth shut," he teased. "That Yankee accent's a dead giveaway."

The drive took them back along the road they had traveled that morning, until they reached the town of Sanderson. Ryan turned off the highway into a residential section. The houses were set back from the street and spaced to leave large expanses of lawn.

Rosemary marveled at the size of the lots. In New York if there was fifty feet of undeveloped land, someone would figure out a way to put a high-rise on it.

"Stan delivered some papers from the New York office. Before we have dinner I need to drop them off at my comptroller's house," Ryan explained as he parked on a grassy verge in front of a small contemporary bungalow. He reached across to the back seat to retrieve the briefcase he'd tossed there that morning.

Ryan had mentioned his comptroller several times, but he had neglected to mention that she was a stunning, young blonde. When she answered his knock, Rosemary got a glimpse of long bare legs before the two of them disappeared into the house, leaving the door ajar. She wondered if the woman was married.

In a few minutes they reemerged, and the blonde followed Ryan down the steps and across the lawn toward the car. She was even more beautiful up close, Rosemary thought as Ryan opened the car door and leaned forward to introduce them.

"Rosemary, this is Carole Putnam, my comptroller."

"How do you do, Miss Addision?" the young woman said with flattering enthusiasm as she bent to extend her hand across the driver's seat. There was no ring on her finger. "I've always admired your work tremendously. Welcome to Sanderson, and to Ryan Mills." She added the last with a quick grin and toss of her head toward her boss. The glorious hair caught the sunlight as it fell from her shoulder to drape becomingly over the front of her well-filled T-shirt.

Rosemary felt a hundred years old. She returned the handshake with a weak smile. "Thank you," she murmured, taking in every detail of the fresh, open face before her. Lord, she was so *young*!

Carole's skin had a healthy glow, as though she spent a great deal of time outdoors. Her eyes were clear blue and her smile, sincere and appealing.

Rosemary couldn't help but respond, though her own lips felt numb. "I'm happy to be here."

"Y'all have fun," said Carole, straightening and cutting off Rosemary's view of all except the slim hips and georgeous legs. "Eat some barbecue for me."

Ryan said something Rosemary didn't catch, but she heard the trill of laughter in response. "No. Andy and I have decided on pizza tonight."

Andy? *Maybe she is married and just doesn't wear a ring.*

And maybe Andy is her brother, another more pessimistic voice chided.

"My tongue is still burning." Rosemary couldn't hold back the complaint as a stone-faced Ryan opened the door of the Lincoln for her. The neon sign in front of the restaurant turned her blue eyes black. She stepped into the car.

"After all the water you drank? I'm surprised you don't slush when you walk." His tone was clipped; he closed the door with more than a snap, less than a slam.

"The barbecue sauce was hot," she repeated for the hundredth time when he joined her.

He jammed the key into the ignition and turned with a force that threatened to break the tiny piece of metal. "I offered to order you a steak instead," he countered shortly.

"I didn't want to act like a coward in front of your friends." The restaurant had been crowded, so the Madisons had invited her and Ryan to sit with them. A couple in their late fifties, they had devoured the hot dishes without a blink of an eyelash, offering praise to the cook as though he were some kind of deity—and expecting her to agree with them.

Ryan waited until they were out of the crowded parking lot to speak again. "Instead you acted like a martyred parvenue, forced to endure the quaint customs of us provincials."

"I did not!" There was a hint of a pout in Rosemary's voice, and she hated herself for it. She straightened her back against the leather seat. "I did not," she said more reasonably. "It was your idea for me to come to Georgia. I told you I wouldn't fit in. If you don't like the way I act, send me home."

"If I remember correctly, you signed the contract without my laying a hand on you," he grumbled sarcastically. "And you could fit in if you'd let yourself relax."

Rosemary glanced across the seat at him. His jaw was granite hard. Ryan had never been this mad at her before. She was surprised at how much his anger upset her.

Thinking back, she supposed she had acted a bit condescending. But the couple had talked as if New York City was some kind of alien planet, inhabited only by muggers, thieves and prostitutes. And judging by the way the woman had looked at Rosemary when she confessed she didn't *want* to learn to cook, the "parvenue" might have been some sort of deviate.

"I'm sorry, Ryan," she finally told him quietly. "I'll try to do better."

"Dammit, Rosie! There you go again. Don't sound like a scolded child!"

"Well, what do you want me to say?" she exploded again. "Just tell me, and I'll say it! You're acting like someone I've never known."

Ryan took a long breath and let it out slowly. His temper seemed to evaporate with the sigh. If Rosemary's intention was to make him feel guilty, she was doing a first-class job of it.

He had hoped— Hell, what had he hoped? That she would adjust to small-town life the instant her feet touched ground in Georgia? That she would regret her dismissal of him five years ago the moment she stepped off the plane? Was he so egotistical that he wanted her to mourn what she'd missed?

The idea took him by surprise, but he recognized it for what it was, unreasonable and sophomoric. *Be honest Tarleton,* he chided himself. *Five years ago was not the right time for either you or Rosemary.* It appeared that Apple Valley wasn't the right place, either.

"Honey, I'm sorry." He reached across the seat for her hand and tugged her closer. Rosemary scooted over until her shoulder was touching his. Taking his eyes off the road for a minute, he smiled down at her. "You've always been an independent type. I should have realized you'd be feeling insecure."

Rosemary opened her mouth to deny his accusation; it seemed to hint at immaturity on her part. But she *was* feeling insecure. She would adjust to life here while she was here, but the sooner she finished this job and got back into her element, the better off she'd be. Perversely, for some reason that thought saddened her. Rosemary was silent for the rest of the ride, remembering her positive outlook of that morning, wondering what had happened to it.

Ryan stopped the car in the cottage driveway and turned off the ignition. Before she could move away his arm swung over her head to hold her next to him.

Surprised, she tilted her head back to look up

into his face. There was an expression there she couldn't read. Slowly she relaxed; tentatively she let her head rest on his muscular shoulder, though she kept her eyes glued to his, waiting.

"Are you tired?" he asked. It was more of a conversational gambit than a request for information, and she recognized it as such.

"A little. It's been a big day."

A half smile played across his lips. He touched her cheek, looped a strand of dark hair behind her ear. "A very big day."

"Ryan, I really am sorry if I offended your friends."

"Forget it. Maud Madison is a stuffed shirt, anyway."

"I thought a stuffed shirt was a term used to describe a man."

He grinned. "Did you see who wears the pants in that family?"

She laughed softly, and then was quiet, examining her hands linked loosely in her lap. "Well, I suppose I should go inside."

"Yes, you should."

She was surprised at his grim tone. Ryan looked deeply into her eyes for a long minute while she held her breath, waiting.

Finally he broke the eye contact, removed his hand from her shoulder and reached for the door handle. Rosemary was flooded with disappointment, shocked to realize she'd been longing for him to kiss her.

She followed him out of the car from the driver's side, the same way she'd done that afternoon, and sauntered in his wake, reluctant to end the evening. They had almost reached the front door when she remembered she hadn't brought a key. "I hope you have an extra key, Ryan. I forgot to look for one before we left."

"The door isn't locked."

"Isn't locked? Are you crazy?"

"Nope. We seldom lock our doors when we go out. Usually only if we're leaving on a long vacation."

"But...all your mother's antiques, Ryan! And the cottage is so isolated...."

"And if a thief is determined do you think he won't find a way to get in?"

The amusement in his eyes stunned her. "Well, you could at least make it difficult for him!"

Tilting his head back, Ryan laughed in obvious delight. "Relax, Rosie. This is a small town. We all look out for one another. The road isn't heavily traveled, and if a strange car was seen the sheriff's deputy would check on it very quickly, believe me."

"Well, you'd better find me a key, because I don't intend to sleep in an unlocked house!"

Casually he took her hand, linking their fingers. "I didn't say anything about when you're inside. Naturally you'll lock up then."

Rosemary shook her head in disbelief at that rationale, but decided she was too tired to try to understand it tonight. Besides, the easy handclasp was drawing all rational thought from her. She had to make a positive effort not to curl her fingers more tightly around his.

They reached the steps, and she mounted the first one, expecting him to move with her. Instead he turned her toward him. The extra height put her face on a level with his.

A waning moon hung in the sky behind his shoulder, shadowing his expression, but she could feel the sudden tension in him. She knew the same light revealed the anticipation she was unable to hide. She wanted to look away, to make some light-hearted, insignificant remark, but it was impossible to break the thread of awareness between them.

He bent his head over her fingers in a lovely, romantic gesture. The brush of his lips across her knuckles caused the air on her nape to rise. Her lids suddenly seemed too heavy; her heartbeat, too slow. And when he turned her hand up to place a tender kiss in her palm, to taste with a flick of his tongue the sensitive skin there, she thought her knees would melt. She swayed with the effort to stay upright. "Ryan, please..."

She had no idea what she was pleading for. A deep, fulfilling kiss? A hard, eager embrace? Or an end to this seductive scene?

With both hands he combed the hair back from her face. His long fingers cradling her head kept her immobile for his thorough study. "Rosie." His voice when he spoke was a beguiling rasp. "I don't know what the hell's happened to me. Believe me when I say I didn't bring you down here for this to happen, but—" he took a long, deep breath "—since you stepped off that plane all I've been able to think of is how much I want to make love to you."

She was so relieved by his admission that she almost laughed out loud. It wasn't one-sided; she didn't have to doubt her own sanity. "Oh, Ryan. I...me, too."

He dropped his hands and linked his arms around her waist, pulling her against him. Their eyes met from a distance of only a few inches. "I hoped you were feeling the same way."

She was off balance, being a step above him, so she wrapped her arms around his neck and let him take her weight. "I have been since I first saw you this afternoon, or maybe it was when you kissed me in the car." Her voice was a husky whisper, but she was amazed she could make a sound at all. "I thought I was imagining that the kiss was different. I mean, you always kiss me...but I've never shivered before."

One large hand slid beneath the hem of her sweater to caress her bare back. His palm was warm against her skin, his fingers spread wide. "I thought I'd gotten over wanting you five years ago. Now all I can think of is how you'd look with your hair spread out on a pillow, how your breasts would taste, how you'd feel naked under me."

"Ryan!" she gasped.

"We've always been honest with each other, haven't we?"

They still stood nose to nose, and she rubbed hers playfully against his. "Honest, yes, but you don't have to put it quite so graphically." A reluctant smile curved her lips.

"That's the way I feel." Raising a teasing brow, he moved his hips suggestively against her. "Graphic."

She hid her face beneath his chin. "I need some time to get used to you," she murmured.

"I know what you mean. I'm on shaky ground, too."

He seemed to want to add something, but not to know how to word it. His being at a loss surprised her, after his quite clear description of what he wanted to do.

"If you ... if we ..." He sighed.

Rosemary raised her head. "If we made love?"

He rested his forehead against hers. "Yes," he said simply. "If we made love and it didn't work out, we'd never be able to go back to the friendship we've always shared."

"I know."

The hand at her back moved restlessly. "So we should think very carefully before we plunge into anything."

"Ryan?"

"Yes, honey?"

"Why don't you shut up and kiss me?"

Smiling, he tilted his head slightly. "I was just

waiting for you to ask." Open and suddenly urgent, his mouth covered hers.

Rosemary thought she knew the meaning of desire, but with the hot, hungry touch of his lips she realized she was greatly mistaken. For the first time in her life her body was completely controlled by passion. With equal hunger she returned the kiss, her tongue demanding more of the taste of him.

Her response turned the kiss into a wild and erotic explosion. The hand at her back came around to cup a full breast. Her body strained against his, her nipple thrusting under the lace barrier into his palm. His mouth roamed over her face and her throat, returning again and again to feast at her lips.

When they broke apart, he looked down at her with an expression of confusion and bewilderment as great as her own. Still breathing heavily, he slowly removed his hand and smoothed her sweater down to cover her midriff.

"I'd better say good night." His voice was thick and husky...and unbelieving.

Rosemary slouched against the door when she reached it, watching through her lashes as he walked away.

5

ROSEMARY SAT ON THE FRONT STEPS, chin propped in her hands, looking balefully at the piece of machinery in the driveway. She knew that as cars went it was small, but to her it looked gigantic and dangerous. And was it ever red! Why would Ryan get her such a conspicuous car?

Her nemesis had been delivered an hour ago, the man's knock rousing her from a deep sleep. She had stumbled to the door, tugging a negligee over her sheer nightgown. His appreciative grin told her she might as well not have bothered. She had scribbled her name on the piece of paper he held out and closed the door smartly in his face.

Mornings were not her favorite times, and now, dressed in beige slacks and a silk blouse of royal blue, she watched and waited like a prisoner at the bar. Sure enough, she didn't have to wait long.

Instead of yesterday's Lincoln, Ryan was driving a red pickup truck. *Matching vehicles, how sweet*, she thought sourly. Was the truck supposed to impress her further with his macho image?

He climbed out and approached, but she didn't give him more than a glance. The brief look was enough for her to get the benefit of his dazzling smile. "Good morning?" he asked her bent head.

Still she stared morosely at his dusty boots. Maybe he intended to simply ignore what had happened between them last night. Well, she couldn't ignore it. The kiss—if such a mild word could apply to a happening like that—had left her extremely upset. She was not accustomed to being upset in that way, and the more she thought about it the more upset she became. Ryan Tarleton had provoked a reaction like none she'd ever experienced. And it scared the hell out of her.

"What's the matter with our city slicker this morning?" he teased, reaching for her hands. He pulled her effortlessly to her feet and into a light embrace. "Did the barbecue not sit well on her sophisticated little stomach?"

It wasn't the barbecue that had kept her awake until dawn. At first it was the kiss; then it was the deathly quiet—that and the memories her foolish mind repeatedly came up with, memories of a young Ryan and younger Rosemary on a Long Island beach, splashing hand in hand through the shallow surf under a golden sun, eating clams and drinking beer, and almost coming to grief in the laundry room.

And then about two o'clock in the morning a chorus of *something* outside her window had begun. It had lasted until daybreak.

Ryan's broad chest was there in front of her, a

temptation, so she laid her head on it. "I didn't sleep very well."

He cupped her head with one broad hand, tilting her chin. "Neither did I," he admitted wryly.

Carefully her gaze slid up past the curve of his mouth to the amused expression in his eyes. He must have just gotten out of the shower. His dark hair was still damp and trying to curl free of its neat brushing, while his clean-shaven cheeks smelled of fine-milled soap. She found her eyes drawn irresistibly back to the sensual mouth and mustache. No! Not again.

She twisted her head to the side. If he didn't plan to mention the kiss, she wouldn't, either. "Ryan, what *were* those things that made such a noise all night? Will they bite?"

Ryan threw back his head and laughed.

Squirming angrily, Rosemary tried to free herself, but his arms only tightened, bringing her in closer contact and making her even more aware of his hard body.

"I think I should warn you that I'm in a rotten mood this morning," she said.

"I noticed." He was still chuckling. When his laughter was spent he laid his cheek on the top of her head. "No, sweetheart, they don't bite." He gave her another of those light little kisses that could have been delivered by any avuncular man without the least offense. This one landed on her forehead. She wrinkled her nose in protest.

"Those are tree frogs," he went on to explain.

"They are about as big as the end of your finger."

She held up the digit and frowned suspiciously. "I don't believe you. Something that small, making so much noise?"

"A few crickets probably lent their voices, too. Come on. Let's see if we can improve your mood." He led her to the new car and opened the passenger door. "I'm going to feed you, and then you'll get your first driving lesson."

"I've had breakfast," she said as she climbed in. The leather upholstery did smell nice, she admitted, and the wood-grained dashboard was attractive. She looked over her shoulder...plenty of room back there for her painting supplies. The only misgiving she harbored about the car was her ability to drive it.

Ryan joined her, folding his length into the other bucket seat. He dismissed her idea of breakfast completely. "Coffee and juice, right?"

She nodded. "That's all I like in the mornings."

"Not today. Today we're having Sunday brunch."

"Are you cooking?" she ask dubiously.

"No, sweetheart. You're safe today. A man who retired from the navy as a cook works for me part-time. You'll like Zack. He's been at the house since six o'clock this morning frying and baking, and stewing a little at the idea of feeding a famous New York designer. He'll be disappointed if you don't eat."

Rosemary's eyes darted to him, but she failed to find any hint of sarcasm in his expression. She shrugged, doubtful that Zack would care one way or the other what she ate, but she didn't argue.

She was learning fast that to argue with Ryan Tarleton in his hometown was of no use whatsoever. He decided she should drive; she would drive. He decided she should eat; she would eat. In New York she may have set the pace of their relationship, but in Georgia he was definitely in charge, and without a good night's sleep to fortify her she didn't have the energy to protest.

Instead she watched carefully as he turned the key in the ignition to start the engine, shifted the gear stick into position and eased the car out of the driveway with a light touch of his boot on the accelerator. That didn't look too hard.

They couldn't have driven much more than a city block when he pulled into a long drive bordered by tall trees with heavy, waxy leaves. The avenue was quite impressive.

"Are these magnolia trees?" Rosemary's natural curiosity was aroused for the first time, and her mood beginning to improve despite herself.

"You're very observant."

"I've seen the leaves used for decoration, but I didn't realize how huge the trees were." Her head swiveled to take everything in. To her surprise she saw that Ryan's home was a working farm.

When he parked and came around to help her out of the car, she realized belatedly that she hadn't watched to see how he had stopped the thing. It couldn't have been too complicated. "Ryan! It's beautiful," she breathed, looking around at the scene and forgetting the car completely in appreciation of the beauty before her.

White Kentucky-style fences dipped and rose to the curve of the gently rolling hills. A huge barn and stables sat at the edge of pastures so green and perfect they looked as though they were covered with some of Ryan's carpet. Cattle grazed placidly in the distance, but in a field abutting the house, beautiful, thoroughbred horses were showing off with a bit more energy. She counted eight of them and three frolicking colts. "How do you **find** time to manage all this?"

He grinned. "The farm is my tranquilizer. I have a manager, but after a day in the boardroom nothing is more relaxing than pitching hay."

A side glance at his powerful physique left her throat slightly dry. The muscles under his white polo shirt were ample testimony of the benefits of pitching.

"It isn't a large holding, only seven hundred acres or so, but I love it. When I retire this is where I want to live."

"I don't understand. You live here now, don't you?"

"Not nearly enough. I still have to travel more than I like," he said without explaining further. He glanced down at the thin gold watch on his wrist and reached for her hand. "We have a few minutes. Come on. I'll show you around."

They walked toward the barn. "Was this your family's farm, too?"

Her question stopped him dead in his tracks. As

he looked down at her his laugh was without humor. "No, Rosemary. We were sharecroppers. Dirt poor. We didn't own anything except the clothes on our backs, and there weren't too many of those."

"But the house...."

"The house you're in? It was built by my great-grandfather. The family lost even that during the depression. This area was devastated first by the war."

She shook her head, not understanding.

"The War Between the States," he elaborated. "Then, just as it was beginning to recover, the depression hit. Now it's a very prosperous part of the country, mainly because of the carpet industry. I bought the house back and had it completely remodeled because my mother had a feeling for it, but I won't ever live there."

A trace of a young boy's pain and struggle was revealed in the vow. For the first time Rosemary understood the extent of Ryan's accomplishments. She had known when they met five years ago that he was well on the way to establishing an empire, but now she was stunned by the scope of his success. How shallow he must have thought her. She had been successful, too, but life had been so much easier on her.

The finest training had been paid for by an indulgent father. She had attended the best schools, but most of all she had been secure in the knowledge that if she failed, her life-style wouldn't change to any great degree. It was a humbling thought. If she had had to fight for her very survival, perhaps she wouldn't have been able to do as well.

To come from absolutely nothing as Ryan had.... what kind of drive and strength and ambition had it taken to amass the fortune he had now? "I'm really impressed, Ryan," she said softly.

As they entered the barn through the wide doors, he turned back to look out over the land for a long, silent minute. He seemed to have forgotten she was there. Then he slid his hands into the pockets of his jeans and faced her squarely. "I owe a lot of it to you," he said, watching her through hooded eyes.

Her eyes flew to meet his, but the sunshine behind his shoulder threw his face into shadow. "To me?"

His gaze roamed over her face for a minute. She stood perfectly still under the scrutiny, almost afraid to breathe lest she snap the thread of his concentration. He was about to divulge some inner feeling, some private part of himself that she'd never known before, and she had to hear, even if his thoughts were censorious.

His eyes had shifted to a point behind her head. "I had enjoyed a certain amount of success before I met you. I got the scholarship, of course, and the plant here was opened on a lot of hope and a local banker's trust. The mill was showing a profit. At that point I went to New York to arrange for expansion financing, and that loan officer, Lawrence Shaw, invited me to his house on Long Island for the weekend.''

That weekend was still a vivid memory, part of what had kept her awake last night.

Ryan's eyes returned to hers. His smile was sad. ''I suppose I thought of myself as invincible, but in only a few days I fell head over heels, as they say. Do you remember?''

Swallowing, she nodded.

''Your father called on Sunday with the letter of acceptance you'd been waiting for. I'll never forget how excited you were.'' He shrugged, leaving much more unsaid. ''All my energies after that went into the business.''

It was the first time Ryan had ever hinted at the depth of pain he had felt when she refused to marry him. Rosemary suspected his words were an understatement. Color crept up her neck. Maybe if he had let her see... She had honestly thought he'd understood the impossibility of a long-term relationship with her.

Tears stung her eyes. She turned away from the sunlight outside and blinked rapidly to clear them as she strolled farther into the shelter of the building. She stared without seeing at the wide, cleanly swept aisle stretching before her. The scents of musty hay and animals, of polished leather and dusty implements, foreign to her, only served to emphasize the contrast between them.

Of course he hadn't understood. She had just

been too immature to recognize the depth of his feelings. Even five years ago, a man of Ryan's stature and pride would have thought carefully before reaching out for a commitment. And a spoiled young woman had flung his tentative feelings back in his face. "Ryan, please..." she whispered.

"It took over a year to get to the point where I could bear to see you again." He spoke from behind her, the words deepening her pain.

She, too, remembered that year. Working to the point of exhaustion and beyond, she had often wondered if success was worth the effort. It had been a desperately lonely time, but her father's encouragement had kept her going. If she'd had another week to spend with Ryan, if her father hadn't called when he did, heaven only knew what would have happened between her and Ryan.

Ryan followed her train of thought with uncanny accuracy. "If you hadn't been accepted I would probably have asked you to marry me again, and been content with the original plant. It would have been a good living."

"But nothing compared to what you have now." She forced a lightness into her voice that she definitely didn't feel, smiling over her shoulder.

He matched his steps to hers. Their shoulders brushed as they ambled along the aisle. "No," he agreed.

"So aren't you glad I had a career to think about?"

"Ecstatic!" He smiled.

His heartiness seemed forced; she couldn't tell,

but she thought so. Or was that just wishful thinking in the wake of discovering new desires? He had said he wanted her, but was his attraction an unconscious form of revenge for past hurts?

"I lost a lover and gained a friend," he added.

They had reached the far end of the aisle. "And made a lot of money," she added, facing him.

"A hell of a lot of money," he concurred quietly. "But the friend will always mean more than any amount of money." An expression of self-derision crossed his face. Still he reached for her hand, holding it securely in his as they began to retrace their steps. "Come on. Let's eat."

The warmth that traveled up her arm to her shoulder helped somewhat to ease the burning sensation in her throat. Their early days as almost-lovers were over, past, but she felt a terrible burden of guilt for hurting him, despite her immaturity at the time. Moreover, she was uncertain about his feelings for her in the present.

"Hey."

She met his eyes.

"It's over," he said gently. "Five years have passed. What we are today, what we might have between us, would be better."

Her relief was overwhelming, but she made herself ask. "Are you sure?"

"I'm positive," he said, sounding that way. "I have no wish to resurrect the tired infatuation of five years ago. I'd rather have the woman than the girl any day."

"I'm glad, because even if I wanted to, I couldn't bring her back." She sighed, a soft sound. "Though the way I've been acting this morning is much more girlish than womanly. I'm sorry, Ryan."

As they stood again on the edge of the sunlight, he murmured, "Rosemary?"

She raised a brow. He never called her Rosemary. "What?"

"Shut up and kiss me."

He reached for her, but she held him off, her hands flat on his chest. "That's how all this started in the first place," she teased unsteadily. "With that kiss last night."

Ryan grinned, suddenly weakened by the sensation of her thighs against his. His hands slid down her back to cradle her hips. "Did you shiver?"

"I most definitely shivered." Her lower body shifted, molding to his in instinctive response. Her arms had found their way around his neck. "Did you?" she whispered, lifting her face.

He shuddered as her breasts came in contact with his chest and inhaled long and deep to strengthen the pressure. His eyes were drawn to her mouth, lingering there. Her lips were pink and moist, enticing him. "I don't even remember how I got home," he confessed hoarsely as he lowered his head.

THE HOUSE was a simple Georgian style with high ceilings and large rooms. Surprisingly, the furnishings were haphazard, placed for convenience only and slightly jarring to the eye. Ryan didn't seem to have put much thought to the inside of his home.

"While you're here, Rosie, you might think about suggestions for this house. I've never quite gotten around to decorating it the way it should be done."

The designer in her responded to the offer without hesitation. "I'd love to. It's a beautiful house. May I have carte blanche?"

Ryan laid an arm across her shoulders. "You may do anything you like."

"I might just lend you some of those antiques I have stored in New York. They would fit in nicely here."

Did the arm around her shoulders become tense, or was that her imagination? Had she said something wrong? She looked up, but he was smiling.

"You'd better keep those things," he said lightly. "You might decide to remodel."

The tension was certainly gone now, replaced by a mysterious glimmer in his eyes that wasn't hard to interpret. The kiss they had just shared had taken their relationship to a higher level of sensuality. She still needed more time, but she didn't even have to ask for it. Somehow they had communicated the same message without words: Slowly this time around.

Ryan steered her through a door beneath the circular staircase into a cheerful morning room where a table was set for two. After seating her he headed for another door. "I'll tell Zack we're ready."

Rosemary stared through tiny panes of glass to a broad veranda that ran the length of the house. If the timing had been right for them, she might have been here in this house with Ryan. Perhaps one or two children would be sharing the table.

Instinctively she knew that had that happened, the result would have been disaster. She would have been settling for security over the challenge of a career. The fires of ambition would have undoubtedly flamed again, fanning her dissatisfaction into resentment, against Ryan and against the marriage. No, it hadn't been the right time. Ryan realized that, too, thank goodness. Mentally she shook herself, jerking her thoughts back to the present.

Zack had hair the color of newly minted silver and an imperturbable disposition, as Rosemary soon discovered. He smiled a guarded welcome in response to Ryan's introduction, then set a steaming platter of bacon, sausages and ham in front of Rosemary. Two more trips produced a bowl of fresh fruit, scrambled eggs and a delicious-looking cheese souffle. "I'll bring the biscuits in a jiffy and pour your coffee. Is there anything else you'd like, Ryan?"

"It looks like you've thought of everything, Zack. I just hope Miss Addison is as hungry as I am."

"It all looks delicious." Rosemary added her own praise. She was surprised to find she was starving. The country air must be giving her such a strong appetite.

Ryan passed the eggs and souffle, and she

served herself generous portions. He chuckled at the sight of her heaping plate. "Zack's breakfasts are hard to resist even when you're not hungry, aren't they?"

Rosemary nodded, her fork already on its way to her mouth with a bite of the souffle. Ryan seemed to be watching for a reaction, but when she hesitated he smiled encouragingly, and she took the bite.

Her eyes widened. The consistency wasn't souffle-like. She moved her tongue against it. Whatever, it was strange, soft and light like souffle, but rather... gritty. Her brows soared as she swallowed.

Biting back a laugh, Ryan took the bread basket from Zack, who had reappeared, and helped himself before setting the basket at Rosemary's elbow. He wasn't trying very hard to control his shaking shoulders when the older man, having filled Rosemary's cup with steaming coffee, asked, "How do you like my cheese grits?"

Rosemary was still swallowing. "They're quite... different," she finally managed, and Ryan let loose the laugh.

"Now, Ryan," Zack scolded, "don't you make fun." He patted Rosemary's shoulder sympathetically. "Grits takes some gettin' used to," he pronounced as he left the room.

Fixing her host with a baleful glare, Rosemary muttered, "You might have warned me."

"And missed the expression on your face? Uh-uh."

Shaking her head as if to suggest he was a hopeless case, Rosemary reached for a biscuit.

RYAN LEANED ACROSS to buckle her seat belt securely. "Now," he said, indicating the key, "this is the ignition. This is the—"

Rosemary interrupted impatiently. "Ryan, I'm not totally stupid. I do know the parts of a car, just not how to drive one!"

Leaning back in his seat, he shrugged. "Okay. Start the engine."

She did what she had seen him do with the key, and the car purred to life. She smiled a satisfied smile. "Now what?" she asked confidently.

AN HOUR LATER Rosemary was covered with perspiration, her blue silk blouse plastered to her back. Her hands ached from gripping the steering wheel, and her right leg shook with uncontrollable spasms.

Ryan had a growing lump on his forehead and a permanent scowl on his face. He had fastened her seat belt but neglected to buckle his own.

"Well, if you wouldn't yell at me..." she said defensively.

"If you weren't so bullheaded..." he answered back through clenched teeth. "Ease your foot onto the accelerator! *Ease*, for God's sake! You're not going for the Indy 500!"

"Damn you!" Rosemary took a deep, shuddering breath, and eased as though there were an egg beneath her toe. The car moved gently forward. She threw a surprised glance at Ryan.

"Keep your eyes on the road!" he roared.

She blinked and obeyed.

"Here comes a car, poor bastard." His fingers gripped the padded dashboard. "Rosemary, stay on your side of the road!"

In response to the command, she twisted the steering wheel convulsively. One wheel of the car left the pavement. The rear end swiveled heartstoppingly into the path of the oncoming vehicle, but the driver managed to avoid a collision by inches. His hand came down on the horn long and hard, throwing Rosemary into further nervous frenzy.

"Not in the ditch!" yelled Ryan, but it was too late. The nose of the small car dipped as the two front wheels mired in rich red mud.

The engine died.

Ryan emitted a long, colorful string of expletives on a deep sigh and rested his head against the seat back. There was a heavy silence in the car.

Rosemary's hands were still wrapped tightly around the steering wheel. She stared straight ahead, waiting for his fury to erupt.

"Why don't I try to find someone to drive for you?" he finally suggested in a much milder tone than she had expected.

"No!"

"No?"

"I'm going to learn if it kills me," she grated.

"Or someone else," he added tonelessly, rubbing the darkening bruise on his forehead.

She didn't reply.

Ryan heaved another exasperated sigh and opened his door to get out. When Rosemary started to do the same his warning came quickly and sharply. "Watch out for the...mud."

From his expression as their eyes met across the top of the car, she knew he could tell his advice had come too late.

She glanced down to see her feet, disappearing under the thick red ooze. She put her head in her arms on top of the car and groaned.

RYAN PULLED INTO THE DRIVEWAY a few feet from his truck, slammed the gear shift to the park position and got out of the car, pointedly taking the keys with him. "Ouch!" he muttered as his bare feet hit the rough gravel. His mincing step reminiscent of a ballet dancer with blisters, he continued around to the rear of the car.

Rosemary clapped a hand over her mouth to stifle a laugh, which would definitely *not* have been appreciated right then. She didn't know where the laugh had come from, anyway.

Back at the scene of the crime, there had been nothing funny about Ryan's curses as he pushed the small car back onto the road, no amusement in his voice when he had instructed her curtly to get in on the passenger's side. There had been nothing funny about his expression when he had looked down at her muddy footprints on the carpet of the new car.

He had clenched his jaw, then pointedly removed his boots to put them in the back before taking over the driver's seat. Rosemary had hastily pulled off her shoes then, but the damage had already been done.

Now he lifted the hatchback and retrieved his mud-caked boots. "I'll pick you up for work in the morning at eight o'clock," he growled, tossing the boots into the bed of his pickup. He paused. "Are you hungry?" he said grudgingly.

"In the middle of the afternoon? No," she answered shortly.

He opened his mouth to say something else, but before he could get any words out she interrupted, "I'll see you in the morning."

She sat where she was, making no move to leave the car. The motor of the pickup grumbled into life even before she heard the door bang. She thought she saw him hesitate again for a second before he threw the truck into gear and roared off.

I didn't really scream at Ryan like that, did I? Only babies and weak, ineffectual adults go into hysterics. Only shrews scream. Was that me?

What was happening? How could two people who were such good friends, who had never exchanged a harsh word in five years, suddenly begin to argue like enemies every time the least little thing went wrong? Remembering the huge lump on Ryan's forehead, she had to admit that wasn't such a little thing. In fact she had to concede that Ryan's patience had held far longer than her own would have with a novice driver screaming like a banshee.

She had offered to fix an ice pack, but it seemed he couldn't wait to get her out of his sight—he would fix his own ice pack. Ryan could have taken the ice from his voice, at least, Rosemary thought. That same man had kissed her so passionately only a few hours earlier, had told her last night that he wanted her, had dreamed of what she would feel like naked. Bosh!

Rosemary dragged herself out of the car toward the house. She needed a shower, clean clothes. But damn—she couldn't have a shower because there wasn't one. She'd be better off in a Holiday Inn. At least there she'd have a choice!

Belatedly it dawned on her that such childishness was unworthy of her. Apologizing meekly to Ryan's absent mother, Rosemary withdrew the thought. Before she reached the steps, however, she veered off the path and circled to the back. The ravine was shady and inviting. Her footsteps made small, crunching sounds as her feet slipped over the blanket of pine needles.

About halfway down the slope she sat, linking her arms loosely around her knees. Birds played in the trees above her head and called gaily to one another. A wayward breeze rustled the blossoms and leaves of the dogwood trees, while some of the larger pine branches creaked an accompaniment to the refrain. She found herself enjoying the sounds and the scents of the forest, and soon the peace of the place began to soothe her ruffled feelings. She rested her forehead on her arms, closing her eyes. "And you thought you were unsettled in New York!" she mumbled into her lap.

Dear heaven, now the man had her talking to herself!

A brief, faint noise that didn't come from a bird brought Rosemary's attention sharply back to her surroundings. Her head came up with a jerk, and halfway fearful she looked around, but saw nothing. She heard the noise again. Not only wasn't it a bird, it wasn't the soft sigh of the leaves, either.

Gingerly she stretched out her hand and, taking one leaf between her thumb and forefinger, lifted the lower branch of a small bush to her left. The shadows were so dense underneath that she didn't see the tiny black creature for a minute. When she did, she let out the breath she'd been holding.

It was a kitten, hardly bigger than the palm of her hand. Back arched defensively, it watched her with frightened yellow eyes that took up most of its face.

"Where did you come from?" Rosemary whispered.

The kitten relaxed slightly and cocked its head to the side, studying her warily.

Woman and cat stared at each other for a long minute, neither quite sure what the next step should be. Rosemary had never had a pet of any kind. Her father hadn't been enamored of domestic animals. Once when she had asked for a puppy, he had also explained the impracticality of having one in an apartment in the city. Should she pick it up?

Her next movement was too abrupt. The kitten backed away with a faint cry.

"I won't hurt you," she promised. This time she walked her fingers over the blanket of pine needles, very slowly. A finger touched a tiny paw, and the cat lurched back out of reach, scaring her almost as much as itself. "Poor thing," she soothed softly. "Are you afraid to be out here on your own?" She lifted the kitten with a hand under its middle.

Suddenly an affinity for the tiny creature sprang full-grown in her. The two of them had a lot in common, she decided. She wanted this kitten. If it didn't belong to someone she wanted to adopt it, and if it had an owner she would try to buy it.

Inside the cottage, she set the kitten on the floor. The yellow eyes watched her every movement. Blessing whoever it was who had stocked the pantry so thoroughly, Rosemary took out a can of salmon and reached for the electric opener. She dumped the pink fish into a soup bowl and placed it near him. He eyed the meal warily but didn't move. He was so young, maybe he'd rather have milk. After filling another bowl from a carton in the refrigerator, she stopped again. Should it be warmed?

A knock on the door startled both inhabitants. The door swung open.

"Where the hell have you been?" Ryan's tone was almost conciliatory compared to his choice of words.

Rosemary's jaw went slack. "I...uh..." She wasn't sure she would tell him about the cat. His mother might not like pets any more than her father had.

Ryan looked down at the bowl in her hands. "Dinner?" he asked mildly.

His mood seemed to have improved since their last meeting. His dark hair was still damp from a shower, and through the rather potent smell of salmon, Rosemary caught a hint of soap.

"Hardly my usual fare." She grinned. "I was walking in the woods. Look what I found."

Ryan smiled. "She's cute," he said, dismissing the meowing kitten.

"She? Is that what it is? I thought it looked more like a he."

Ryan bent to scoop the kitten into his large hand. "You're right. It is a he." He put the animal down and gave it a gentle nudge toward the salmon, then relieved her of the milk bowl. "Contrary to popular belief, milk isn't all that good for cats or kittens."

Now he could face down the moment of panic he had felt when Rosemary hadn't answered the telephone. His throat had gone so dry that if she had answered he couldn't have spoken. All sorts of pictures had flashed through his mind, pictures of things that would be more likely to happen in New York than in Apple Valley.

"I called to apologize to you for losing my temper. I'm ashamed that my patience doesn't seem to have improved any since I taught that girlfriend of mine in high school," he said.

Remembering how she'd thought he was being unduly cautious with all his warnings, she wasn't particularly proud of herself, either. She recovered quickly. "That's all right. I understand. I wasn't exactly the most cooperative pupil."

They both watched the kitten pick daintily at his dinner. "I'd like to keep him if you don't think your mother would mind," said Rosemary. "I've never had a pet, and I'll enjoy the company."

"Mother wouldn't mind." His tone was easygoing. "I'll ask around, but you can probably keep him if you want to."

"Thank you. Shall we go into the living room?"

Ryan followed Rosemary. She looked like a barefoot urchin with her slacks rolled up like that. Her blouse had come untucked from the waistband, and her ankles were still smeared with mud. Her hair had escaped from the scarf she had tied around it when the driving lesson began. Ryan frowned. The driving lesson. He had behaved like a damned fool, snapping and yelling at her. What was wrong with him? He had never lost his temper with Rosemary before. But then, he thought with a wry grin as he watched her hips sway slightly in front of him, this certainly wasn't the Rosemary Addison who resided on Fifth Avenue, either.

"Have you really never had a pet of any kind?" he asked in a strange tone as she took a seat.

"No, I haven't." She made herself laugh at his obvious look of pity. "Honestly, Ryan. I wasn't deprived!" She clamped her teeth onto her lower lip, but not before the words were out. Strangely, she never thought about Ryan's background when he was in New York, but here her sympathies were definitely aroused. The idea of the boy Ryan had been, having to work like a man, saddened her.

"And you think *I* was, don't you?" he continued for her. He came to stand beside her.

She looked up into his eyes, her expression wary, afraid she had hurt him.

"Don't watch what you say with me, Rosie. That was a long, long time ago." He smiled gently, and she relaxed. "Besides, I *always* had a pet. Now would you like to go somewhere for dinner? I'm afraid my previous invitation was rather inhospitable."

"Grudging is the word," she taunted lightly. "I...I still have to wash off this mud, though, so I think I'll just have a sandwich tonight if you don't mind, Ryan. And an early night." The words came out in a nervous rush.

"I'll see you in the morning, then." When he reached the door to the kitchen he hesitated for a minute. "What are you going to call Butch, here?"

Her eyes followed his gaze to where the kitten sat at his feet, his little stomach rounded like a small, replete Buddha.

"Butch is a good name," she decided.

Ryan nodded. "Good night, Rosie. Let's hope we both sleep better...."

She wasn't sure she liked the wicked twinkle in his eye.

6

"CHARLES DAVIS was born a pessimist," Ryan told Rosemary the next morning on the way to the mill. "He's a firm believer in Murphy's Law, but don't let that fool you. He's also a genius at carpet design."

She looked beyond Ryan's profile to the trees flying past. This morning, under dense cloud cover, the startling green that she was beginning to associate with spring in Georgia had dulled to drab olive. Her misgivings returned with the influence of the overcast day. "What will Charles Davis think about having a raw beginner thrust on him?" she wondered aloud.

"Hey, don't worry." He reached across the seat between them for her hand. "You're far from a raw beginner," he said, entwining their fingers.

"I feel like one." She returned his smile, but her effort was weak, as weak as her response to his kiss when he had picked her up a short while ago. He had seemed to sense her nervousness and didn't force the issue.

Although she was self-confident as a rule, Rosemary always felt this helpless disquiet whenever she began a new project. The feeling usually lasted only until she had actually begun, but during the days, the hours just preceding, she was sure the ideas would vanish, the creative juices dry up. Yes, she definitely felt like a raw beginner.

Ryan lifted her hand to brush his lips over her knuckles. "Relax, honey. You look very professional this morning. And very beautiful."

Even the compliment failed to distract her. She smoothed the lapel of the gray linen blazer with a restless hand. "Thank you," she murmured automatically.

He chuckled. "You're welcome." Not releasing his grasp, he lowered their clasped hands to the seat between them.

"I don't know why I ever let you talk me into this," she grumbled. "But I'll be all right as soon as I start to work. Tell me more about Mr. Davis."

"Well, first he'll probably call in experts to confirm my sanity," Ryan teased. "When Karistan hired Halston to design a line of carpet, Charles ranted for days. He was convinced they had lost their minds. He swore that no plan for distribution, no matter how cost efficient, could compensate for the expense. He was terrified that they had set a dangerous precedent, and that they'd all lose their shirts."

His teasing didn't calm her trepidation. "Did they?" she asked hesitantly.

"Set a precedent? Yes. Several others have used

the idea, and now I've joined the list," he commented cheerfully.

"I meant did they lose their shirts?"

His hand left hers to return to the steering wheel. He hesitated for a minute, but since he had put on his signal for a left turn, she couldn't be sure the pause wasn't automatic. "I understand that King's Ransom lost quite a bit, but it's not known to be a particularly well-run company. My comptroller wouldn't stand for a project that wasn't cost effective."

"Good. You need someone to protect you from yourself. You only offered me this job because you were worried about me, didn't you? You wanted to get me out of New York for a while."

He laughed. "Honey, you mean a lot to me, but I wouldn't let my company go bankrupt on a whim, I promise you."

"I didn't think you would go that far, but I'm glad to hear you confirm it," she told him primly. "And I want to thank you for bringing the supplies for my kitten." Ryan had arrived that morning with a box of kitty litter and a case of catfood.

"Where did you get all that stuff so early in the morning?"

"Nicholson's Feed and Seed opens at six-thirty. Farmers get up early in the country, Rosie."

"I hope he'll stay with me."

"He'll stay. Not every cat has the opportunity to live in a house where they feed you salmon!"

RYAN MILLS was a huge complex, including mill, trucking barn and offices. It covered fourteen acres, Ryan told her as he parked the Lincoln in an assigned spot.

The next hour was a kaleidoscope of people and color, high-tech and bustle. Yet another facet of Ryan Tarleton became part of that shifting pattern.

He insisted on showing her around himself, and in the space of sixty minutes it was obvious he was an understanding employer, a hard-headed businessman, not to mention a sometime mechanic.

They had just finished a tour of the showrooms and entered the mill itself when a stream of curses, heavily seasoned with a Scottish burr, greeted them. Ryan grinned. "That's MacDonald, the plant manager— Hey, Mac! What's up?" Ryan had raised his voice to a level audible over the clacking and groaning of a gigantic piece of machinery.

From somewhere in its depths a face appeared, smeared with grease. "Ho, Ryan! Can you give me a hand?" The face disappeared.

Without hesitation Ryan shrugged out of his jacket, handing it to Rosemary. He quickly released the cuffs of his shirt and rolled them to his elbows. "Hold on a minute, Rosie," he said loudly; then he, too, disappeared.

While she waited Rosemary looked around at the exotic scene. Some of the machines were as large as a building, and so huge that the workings appeared to be reachable only by stairs. Acres of carpet in various stages of completion spewed from each.

A man smiled at her and politely doffed his cap as he drove by in a small, strange-looking vehicle. It resembled a golf cart except for the long shaft extending straight out in front of the driver. He returned a moment later with a roll of carpeting speared on the long metal finger and saluted her again.

Her ears were beginning to ring from the noise by the time Ryan returned to her side. He was grinning like a small boy, and there was a smear of grease on his cheek. With a nod of his head he indicated the direction they should take while he rolled down and rebuttoned his cuffs.

Once the door to the mill was closed behind them, Rosemary was shocked by the sudden quiet of the hall. Taking his jacket from her, he shrugged into it. "Everything has to be soundproof," he explained as they proceeded down the corridor.

"Wait a minute." She glanced up at him and stopped. Reaching into his breast pocket, she took out his handkerchief to wipe at the grease on his face. "Did you get your machine fixed?"

"Mac had everything under control. He was just trying to make me feel needed." He grinned in self-depreciation. "The design studio's down that way," he told her as they passed another corridor. But when she would have turned he took her elbow. "I want you to see my office first."

Ryan's office was in a corner of the building with windows on two walls; it gave a view of green rolling hills. The room was large but sparsely decorated, an office meant for working rather than impressing. She hadn't taken more than two steps inside when she heard the door close, felt his arms come around her from behind.

"I just want you to myself for one minute before I show you where you'll be working," he murmured into her hair.

Rosemary let herself settle against him, and his arms tightened. "That wasn't a very enthusiastic kiss you gave me earlier. I don't know how I'm going to get through this day, knowing you're so close."

"Ryan, you promised..."

"We both need time, I know, but dammit, Rosie, I lay awake half the night thinking about making love to you."

She turned in his arms, linking her hands behind his back. "So did I."

Rosemary only had a glimpse of his gorgeous, smoky eyes before his lids fell to hide them and his mouth covered hers.

The kiss had barely begun when they were separated by a gasp of surprise. "I'm sorry," muttered the embarrassed woman. "I didn't know you were in, Ryan. Jackie said—"

"It's okay, Carole. Come in." Calmly Ryan dropped his arms from around Rosemary.

Carole recovered her equilibrium with admirable speed, but she was obviously shaken. The papers she had been carrying were clutched to her chest.

Rosemary wondered whether her shock came

from seeing someone when she expected an empty office, or from the sight of a passionate embrace. Carole didn't leave her much time to speculate.

"How are you, Miss Addison?" she responded with a smile.

"Great, thank you," she murmured, taking in every detail of the younger woman's slim, burgundy-clad figure. The suit was the latest thing in up-and-coming career woman apparel. Yet it did nothing to hide Carole's feminine curves, nor did it detract from the glowing skin and appealing smile that Rosemary remembered from their first meeting.

Rosemary blanched at the memory of Carole's face as she'd come through the door. Was Carole something special to Ryan? Her heart took a plunge at the thought.

"Are those for me?" Ryan asked. "Just leave them on my desk, okay? I'll take a look when I get back." His hand at her back urged Rosemary toward the door.

His comptroller looked as though she might argue, then changed her mind. "Okay."

Ryan introduced Rosemary to his secretary, but hustled her out so quickly that she barely had an impression of steel-gray hair and a disapproving frown.

"Ryan! The mail," Jackie called impatiently.

"I'll be back in a few minutes, Jackie." He tossed the comment over his shoulder to the protesting woman.

"She's a martinet, but I couldn't get along without her," he explained.

They passed several open doors. "Carole seems awfully young to have such a responsible position," Rosemary ventured, wanting to know more about the beautiful blonde but not wanting to ask directly.

"She's twenty-seven." Ryan shot her a glance that held amusement.

"Really? That old? She looks much younger."

"Yes, she does, doesn't she?" Ryan murmured.

Rosemary couldn't tell whether his tone was indifferent or offhand.

A man approached them from the other direction. He was almost as tall as Ryan and very distinguished. As he drew near, Rosemary could see the sharp gleam of intelligence in his eyes. He smiled, and she returned the smile. "This must be Miss Addison," he said.

"Rosie, this is Paxton Norwood, the executive vice-president of Ryan Mills. He's not only my right hand, he's my whole arm, and my very good friend."

"I'm happy to know you, Mr. Norwood," she said, holding out her hand.

"Please call me Paxton. You'll find out that everyone's on a first-name basis around here."

"And I'm Rosemary."

The man turned to Ryan. "Will you be free soon? I'm afraid we have a bit of a problem brewing."

Ryan frowned, his relaxed stance suddenly grown tense. "In Birmingham?"

"Right."

Unconsciously he tightened his hand at Rosemary's elbow. "Damn! I'll meet you in your office in five minutes. Just let me take Rosemary to the studio and introduce her to Charles."

Her legs were straining to keep up with him, but she didn't complain. It was obvious from Ryan's abrupt distraction that something was wrong. The introductions were made quickly, and Charles Davis watched as Ryan turned to her. He took her shoulders in a firm grasp. "I hate to leave you, Rosie. I meant to stay until you felt comfortable but—"

Rosemary interrupted. "Don't worry about me, Ryan," she urged reassuringly. "Go take care of your problem. I'll be fine."

"Charles will show you last season's samples, and I'll try to see you for lunch." He touched her arm in a gentle gesture that was somehow as affecting as a kiss on the cheek would have been. Looking down at her sleeve, she thoughtfully fingered the material. She watched bemusedly as Ryan disappeared around a corner, until her rather dreamy state was interrupted by a sharp "Ahem."

Her brows rose in surprise as she turned to Charles. She had never heard anyone actually say "Ahem" before. It was difficult to smile past her feelings of trepidation, but she managed.

Charles took her into the studio, which was large and brightly lit, and introduced her to the other four people in the room. Three women and one man greeted her with a fair amount of curiosity and a hint of suspicion before returning to their tasks.

Rosemary looked around as Charles gave a few terse orders. The floor was littered with samples of carpet in all phases of design, from tempera-colored drawings on graphs, to silk screen, to cloth strikes in sepia, to finished designs. One entire wall was a continuous drawing board with a number of high stools at angles.

Rosemary mentally rubbed her hands together.

DURING THE COURSE of the morning she discovered that Ryan's description of Charles Davis had been apt if understated. The man habitually wore the most woebegone expression she'd ever seen. He rarely talked, and when he did his voice was clipped and short. But he knew his business. And he assumed that she knew hers, which was flattering.

Lunchtime arrived before she knew it.

Charles approached her almost reluctantly. "Ahem, Rosemary, several of us usually go to a restaurant nearby for lunch. Would you like to join us today?"

The invitation wasn't the warmest, but that was the most number of words he'd strung together all morning, and Rosemary swiveled on her stool to stare at him. "How kind of you, Charles. But I suppose I'd better wait for Ryan."

He bowed rather formally and left.

I hope I haven't offended him, she thought, returning to her study of last season's designs.

Except for the occasional ringing of a telephone, the noise in the building settled to a background drone. Rosemary hummed softly to herself. A swatch board of color predictions for next year in her left hand, she reached for a pencil and began to doodle on a sheet of drawing paper. Colors, colors…there was still something in the back of her mind that niggled at her. And it concerned colors.

She didn't know when she became aware that someone was watching her, but when the tingle between her shoulder blades persisted, she spun around. "Ryan. How long have you been there?"

He lounged against the doorjamb with his hands in his pockets. His tie was loosened, the top button of his shirt open. "A minute," he answered, and stood upright. "Having fun?" he asked with a grin, though his expression was troubled. "I thought you'd have gone to lunch when I didn't show up."

"I really wasn't hungry. Have you eaten?"

He shrugged. "I'll just get a sandwich from the vending machine. I can't leave the plant until a call I'm expecting comes through." He wandered around the studio touching a swatch here, a sample there, moving restlessly.

"Is something wrong, Ryan?" she finally asked.

"Yeah." He sighed tiredly, rubbing his nape. "I'm probably going to have to fly to England tomorrow or the next day. We have a threat of a strike in one of our operations over there."

"Oh. That Birmingham."

"That one," he confirmed with a smile. As he passed her stool he reached out to touch her cheek with a fingertip. "Hey, have you tried out any of the computers yet?"

"Heavens, no. I'm just trying to learn my way around."

He stopped in front of a screen and turned on the power. It began to glow immediately. "Come over here."

She slid off the stool. He picked up a wand that looked like a fat ball-point pen and touched its tip to the screen. A dot appeared. He was grinning like a small boy with a new toy. "Watch this."

"Rosie," he scrawled across the screen. Then he drew a stick flower that in no way resembled a rose. Touching a few buttons, he varied the color on the screen.

"Ryan! That's amazing. I've seen computers used in other areas of design, but I didn't know you could use them for carpet. Can you scale it?"

He touched another button, and a grid appeared behind his design. After adjusting the size of the word on the screen, he typed in a final command. "Now for a demonstration of the marvels of electronics."

The computer told him to wait, while a whirring noise seemed to be concentrated to the left side of the keyboard. When the sound ceased he unplugged a tiny square of plastic and held it up for her to see. "This is a design chip. Take it back to the mill and put it in the right machine, and it will produce carpet with this design and this color. We seldom use it except for special orders." He pocketed the chip and took her hand. "Come on. I'll buy you lunch. Would you prefer bologna or liverwurst, my lady?"

His hand was warm around hers, sending sensual responses to her brain and her heart. Despite his cheerful demonstration he looked so worried that Rosemary had an overwhelming urge to wrap her arms around him. Her casual tone was forced and unnatural. "Goodness, such a choice. No peanut butter?"

He caught the timbre immediately. "I wish I could take you to England with me," he said suddenly, quietly. His arm curved around her shoulders to pull her close.

"How long will you be away?"

"At least two weeks."

She didn't want Ryan worrying about her. He had enough worries, if his plant in England was on the verge of a strike. She leaned into him, her body language saying what she couldn't admit aloud; that under other circumstances she would have loved to be with him. "We both know my job is here, Ryan—as long as you can arrange a temporary driver for me," she joked.

The words were barely out of her mouth when his other arm came around to crush her close, and his mouth sought hers. She was beginning to anticipate her reaction and returned the kiss with all the fiery warmth that flooded through her. His hand tangled in her hair, cupping the back of her head, while his mouth devoured hers.

Finally he broke off the kiss. He was breathing like a long-distance runner as he tucked her head under his chin. "Good point," he said hoarsely. "I'll make sure you'll be taken care of, honey." His voice trailed off to a whisper as he inhaled the scent of her hair.

"I'll be here, Ryan," she said softly. "I'll be here for you when you get home." The words were spoken like a promise, a vow that surprised even her with its intensity.

"What a time for you to tell me that!" he groaned, his hands holding her hips, his body moving spontaneously against her. "You must know how much I want you, Rosie."

Ryan felt as if he was about to leave the planet. Rosemary was so soft and warm, so good, so very good and right in his arms. No woman had ever had this effect on him, not even in those days of raw, burgeoning manhood. Some remnant of sanity held, however, and he finally managed to gain a modicum of control. With his hands at her waist, he lifted her onto her stool. "Stay there. I'll get us a sandwich," he said hoarsely, and escaped.

His hand slid into his pocket for change, and he found the small computer chip. He fingered it absently for a minute, then turned to push through the door to the floor of the mill.

What was he going to do about his feelings, Ryan asked himself as he fed quarters into the machine a few minutes later. He could not, would not, fall in love with Rosemary. Not again. And if he did, he added silently, not realizing the irrationality of his thoughts, he would not ask her to marry him. She would most certainly say no, and then where would he be?

"Here we go. I didn't realize how hungry I was. Ham and cheese okay?"

"Sure." Rosemary's smile was determinedly cheerful.

Hitching a hip onto the stool next to her, Ryan handed her the sandwich along with a package of potato chips and a can of cola. He unwrapped his own sandwich and took a hungry bite before opening his own flip-topped can.

She nibbled slowly, watching him as he ate, thinking absently that it must take a lot of fuel to keep that large body going. The other half of her sandwich was offered and accepted.

When he'd finished eating he took the last swallow from the aluminum can and tossed it into the trash basket beneath the drawing board. "I have a surprise for you," he said as he gathered up the papers and tossed them away, too.

"A surprise?"

He nodded and grinned, seemingly very pleased about something. "If I'm not mistaken I hear it coming now."

The burly Scotsman from that morning filled the door. Ryan crossed the room to meet him.

"Here you go, Ryan," he said, handing his boss a

short, rolled-up piece of carpeting. "It turned out pretty good, for an amateur designer."

"Thanks, Mac."

MacGregor tipped his cap. "Miss Addison," he said politely, and was gone.

Ryan held one end of the roll and let the other fall free. "How do you like it?" he asked, dropping the other end and standing back to observe her reaction.

Rosemary's smile widened in wonder at the surprise. She slid off the stool, kneeling down on the floor at the edge of the piece of carpeting.

Her palm ran lightly over the thick, rose-colored pile. She traced her name and the silly flower in pink with a finger tip. The length of the carpet had been cut off to a narrow strip, but the width must have been about twelve feet, so that there were three repeats of the design. "I love it, Ryan! Lord, what possibilities! It's unbelievable. Why, less than an hour ago..."

"I told you, didn't I?" He couldn't keep the pride and pleasure out of his voice.

Hurriedly she got to her feet, throwing her arms around his waist in an enthusiastic hug. "Yes, you told me, but the demonstration is so much more effective."

"And what kind of demonstration would you be wanting, my dear?" he said, with an attempt at MacGregor's accent.

She giggled. "I believe we sound more Irish than Scottish, but what the heck? What kind of demonstration would you be offering, sir?"

A throat-clearing sound separated them.

"Rather expensive demonstration, isn't it, Ryan?" Charles asked from the door to his office. He frowned at their smiling faces.

Ryan's eyes narrowed. "It's my money, Charles," he said in a quiet tone that nevertheless carried a definite warning.

7

"Do you like it? Really?" asked Carole as she pirouetted in front of the mirror. Yards of pale-blue silk chiffon billowed around her ankles.

Rosemary smiled. "I really do," she told the younger woman. "The color is perfect on you."

"And you don't think it's too much for Saturday night at Barbecue Heaven?"

Both women giggled, and the snuff-colored eyes of the saleswoman who hovered nearby reflected her horror. The Atlanta shopping trip had begun as an exercise in driving for Rosemary. But the day was turning out to be fun.

Apparently before Ryan had left he had alerted everyone in the business to welcome Rosemary and make her feel at home. Carole had taken over the driving lessons, which was a definite improvement over Ryan. In two days the younger woman had Rosemary driving on the highway. On the fourth day Carole had gone with her, offering moral support when she took the test for a license.

The written test was a breeze. She had had some trouble on the driving part, but the young highway patrolman had soon put her at her ease, after which she passed with flying colors.

In the process she and Carole had become fast
friends.

"You'll find a place to wear it, Carole," Rosemary
assured her now. "I knew when we saw that work
of art in the window it was your dress."

"I suppose if I don't get to wear it before, I can
always save it for the Christmas party. Every year
Ryan brings the office personnel down here to the
Ritz-Carlton for a dinner dance."

The smile faded from Rosemary's face. She rose
and strolled over to a display of scarves, fingering
the silken fabrics with an air of interest so Carole
wouldn't see the sudden sadness she knew was in
her expression. By the time Christmas arrived she
would be long gone, back to her life in New York.
She glanced at her watch. "We're supposed to meet
Jackie at the restaurant in half an hour. I'm starved.
Aren't you?"

Carole didn't reply for an awkward minute.
"Yes, shopping makes me hungry," she said finally.
"I'll hurry and change."

Rosemary felt guilty then for interrupting Carole's shopping. The restaurant was in the mall,
anyway. "We aren't in that much of a rush," she
quickly added. "Was there something else you
wanted to try?"

The saleswoman came forward.

Carole laughed. "I'd love to try everything in the
shop. But I'm afraid my plastic money card will
melt if I put any more on it today." She turned to
the woman. "I'll take this dress."

"Certainly, madam," the woman said, her manner stiff. "Will this be cash or charge?" The question was standard but delivered in a tone that plainly said not to try to put anything over on *her*.

"Charge," said Carole, biting her lip as she made a face at Rosemary. "I'll just get myself out of the dress, shall I, while you check my credit?" she added sweetly.

Carole handed her the card, and the woman had the grace to look embarrassed when she took it.

"Back in a jiffy," Carole said to Rosemary as she disappeared into the dressing room.

Watching her go, Rosemary bit back a smile and shook her head.

Carole's exact relationship with Ryan was still a mystery, but Rosemary didn't believe it was a romantic one. Or maybe she just didn't want to believe it. In any case, Carole was intelligent, witty and mature, yet her attitude toward Ryan, which was close to hero worship, sat rather oddly on a woman her age.

Hero worship didn't describe his secretary's attitude, Rosemary mused as she turned from the display of scarves and went back to the low chair where she had left her own packages.

Jackie truly admired Ryan. Her initial reserve toward Rosemary had turned to guarded good will. When he had telephoned from England the first day, he had stayed on the line while Jackie raced to the studio to call Rosemary to the phone. After that Jackie began notifying Rosemary as soon as the

calls came through. And commiserating with her
when they had stopped three days ago.

"He's probably in nonstop meetings. There's always the time difference, too," the secretary had
said consolingly that morning on the way to Atlanta. "And he was going to try to take a day to
visit his new nephew." Beth, Ryan's sister, had
given birth the day he'd arrived in England.

He could call me at home, Rosemary had thought
at the time, but she hadn't said that to Jackie. She
hadn't been sure how the conversation was affecting Carole, and besides, she had needed to concentrate on her driving.

Jackie was waiting for them when they arrived at
the restaurant. She smiled at the load of packages
they both carried. "Good heavens! I didn't know it
was possible to buy so much in two hours," she
said, holding up her own purchase, one small bag.

"Don't look at me," Rosemary defended herself,
laughing as she deposited the packages in a corner
behind the table. "These are all Carole's things."

"Ah, but I was guided by a pro. The next time I
admit to having no color sense I'll be careful. But,
Jackie, wait till you see me at work next week. I'll
knock your socks off. It's absolutely astonishing.
Rosemary can look at a dress or suit, and she
knows instantly whether it's right or not."

By the time Carole finished the breathless speech,
the two other women were laughing. She looked
from one of them to the other. "You laugh, but just
you wait. Even Ryan—" She broke off, her face

flooded with color as she cast a guilty look at Rosemary. Jackie looked uncomfortable, too.

The moment was saved as the waiter approached. He distributed menus, and they ordered lunch. Conversation was resumed, but the gaiety seemed to have gone out of the day for Rosemary. Carole was so right for him, she thought sadly.

ROSEMARY SAT on a high stool, swinging her leg to the rhythmic hum of the air conditioner. Her pencil flew over the sheet of drawing paper. It was after seven, and Ryan Mills was almost deserted. Occasionally she heard the echo of a door closing or muted voices, but she was the only one left in the design department.

The isolation suited her mood. Ryan had been gone for ten days; meanwhile, she was trying to overcome her feeling of abandonment. The reaction was identical to the almost desperate loneliness she'd experienced when he left New York after her birthday. On a rational level she realized that was a ridiculous way to feel, but she couldn't shake the deep yearning for him. Damn him! He had brought her down here. How dare he go off to England the first week.

Straighten up, Rosemary. The trip was an emergency.

Her scowl was gradually displaced by an indulgent smile as she nibbled the end of her pencil and thought of all the invitations and attention she had received since he'd been gone.

Besides Carole's help in learning to drive, Paxton

and his wife, June, had obviously been the ones delegated to make sure she didn't starve. She had been presented with a standing invitation to dinner and had spent one pleasant evening with the couple and their four children.

But when she declined their urging to come often, explaining that she wasn't totally helpless in the kitchen, they alerted Zack. As a result both the freezer and refrigerator in the cottage were crammed with more food than an army could possibly eat.

Rosemary heaved a sigh, tossing her pencil aside, and forced herself to concentrate on the work in front of her. Drawing a long string of colored yarn poms toward her, she studied the samples of the colors predicted to dominate next year's home market. She frowned. There was still something persistently teasing at the back of her mind, some scrap of information she couldn't quite pinpoint. She tucked an errant strand of hair behind her ear and hooked her heel over the bar of the high stool.

Color forecasts were familiar to her, certainly, as they were to every designer. In the fashion industry colors were predicted up to eight years in advance. Occasionally, though, something could happen to negate the predictions, usually something political; or a happening of world-wide importance could have an influence—

"Rosemary." Paxton spoke distractedly from the door of the studio, his voice causing her to jump. He smiled his apology. "I'm glad you're still here. I just had a call from the airport. Ryan's plane will be landing in fifteen minutes—I have to wait around here for a call. Can you pick him up?"

Paxton's unexpected appearance was nothing compared to the jump her heart took at the news that Ryan was only fifteen minutes away. "Sure," she said, proud of the nonchalant tone. "I thought he wasn't due back for a couple of days."

"He must have finished early. I appreciate this, Rosemary."

Ryan is coming, Ryan is coming. She remembered the chant that had buzzed through her mind the night he had come to her apartment in New York, ages, eons ago. She slid off the stool and reached for her purse. Slinging the strap over her shoulder, she sauntered toward the door. "No problem," she told him, her hand on the light switch.

"Thanks. See you tomorrow," said Paxton as he disappeared into his office three doors down the hall.

"Night, Paxton." Rosemary snapped off the lights in the studio. She listened until she heard his inner door click shut; then, her excitement bursting its bounds, she whirled and ran down the dim hallway to the ladies' room.

Five precious minutes later she emerged, her hair freed from the severe bun she had worn all day, vigorously brushed and shining. Her lips were freshly glossed, and she moved in a mist of Joy perfume. The jacket of her suit had been discarded; her fingers toyed with the top button of her Vnecked blouse. Would Ryan be susceptible to a little cleavage?

"Good night, Miss Addison," said the security guard with a smile as he held the door for her. "Have a nice evening."

"I plan to do just that, Paul." She grinned back. "Good night."

She unlocked the EXP and tossed her purse into the back. Before starting the engine Rosemary opened the sun roof. She tried very hard not to think, not to anticipate...anything. The clock on the dash reminded her she had seven minutes left. Plenty of time to drive the short mile to the local airport.

After parking in a darkened corner of the paved lot, she got out of the car and leaned against the fender to wait. Her head fell back to let the moonlight bathe her face. The stars above were like shimmering beads on black velvet, the moon like a gleaming hole in the fabric of the sky. The only sound was the drone of traffic from the interstate highway, out of sight behind a wide band of pine trees, and the throbbing of her pulse in her ears.

Then she heard a muffled murmur from far in the distance. As she listened the murmur became a hum. She searched among the stars until she found the flashing red-and-green lights that were Ryan's plane. The speck in the sky grew slowly; wings took shape; moonlight glinted on the fusilage. Gracefully the plane began its descent.

Rubber touched tarmac, bounced with her heart

and finally settled to earth. The pilot taxied to the edge of the grass. The engines were silenced, while the night seemed to hold its breath along with her. The hydraulic door was lowered, revealing Ryan's broad-shouldered silhouette in the rectangle of light. At last she breathed.

His tie was loose and the top button of his shirt undone. His jacket was looped on two fingers. Slinging it over his shoulder, he picked up his suitcase with the other hand and loped down the steps. He said something to the man who followed him. Deep masculine tones were too faint to be heard, but she recognized his soft laughter. She should step forward, show herself, but for a moment she indulged in watching him secretly.

Then he turned and without hesitation headed directly for where she was standing, as though he felt her presence without seeing her.

Rosemary straightened, unsure if her knees would support her. Ryan walked through a pool of light thrown from one of the tall poles, seemed to hesitate, then plunged into the darkness again. He was ten feet away when he stopped abruptly. "I wasn't sure you'd come to meet me."

His statement surprised her, and she caught her lower lip between her teeth. "Paxton was waiting for a call, but I would have come anyway if I'd known. Didn't you think I would?"

They spoke casually, belying the tension that was airborne between them.

"I asked for you," he said.

"Did you? He didn't tell me that."

Shadows deepened the lines in his face, but the unearthly light from the moon was enough to illuminate the expression in his eyes. The yearning she saw there was a mirror of her own. "Oh, Ryan, I've missed you so," she whispered. She took a step. And then she was hurling herself into the outstretched arms still burdened with luggage.

"Rosie, Rosie," he groaned as he gathered her into a desperate embrace. The suitcase bumped her derriere, but neither of them noticed.

Her arms were wrapped around his neck, her hands hugging her elbows for security, as he lifted her off her feet. Their gazes tangled for a moment on an equal level, and then he laughed joyously, spinning her in his arms, dropping the suitcase. "Rosie!"

His mouth claimed hers with unbridled demand, and she met his need with intense longing and a depth of passion that stunned her. Her senses swam under the onslaught of the scent of him, the taste, the feel of his hard body. Desire for this strong man throbbed in her bloodstream, racing to nourish her veins, her nerves, to a point of sensitivity just before pain.

His lips moved to her temple; his head tilted to give him access to her throat. He covered her face with hungry, stinging kisses, her eyes, her brow, and then returned to nibble at the edge of her mouth. His tongue toyed with her swollen lips and thrust inside to stroke across her teeth. Finally he lifted his head. "Come home with me," he said huskily.

Home...what a nice word. Rosemary thought dreamily that she'd never realized just what a nice word it was, even when it wasn't associated with any particular place. Home was wherever loved ones were. She knew, of course, what her answer would be. Her decision had been made long before tonight. Maybe she had decided while he was gone, maybe when she'd agreed to come to Georgia. Maybe the decision had even been made five years ago—the knowledge buried in her subconscious that someday they would be together.

"Okay," she said carefully. "You drive."

She hadn't realized he'd been holding his breath, waiting for her answer, until he sighed heavily in relief and rested his forehead against hers. He gave her a tight hug. "Nope." Smiling tenderly, he slowly released his arms from around her waist, letting her toes touch the ground. He smoothed the hair away from her face. "I'm tired. You drive."

Her desire was slightly dampened by apprehension. "Are you sure?" She really didn't want to, not with him beside her. And not tonight when her hands were shaking already.

"Honey, I'm really beat. I don't see a chauffeur, so I presume you drove here." His brow rose in inquiry.

She swallowed and nodded. "I have a license now."

He kissed her parted lips. "Good. If the state of

Georgia thinks you're good enough, you can get me home. Let's go." He reached around her and opened the passenger door. Tossing his suitcase and jacket in the back, he climbed in and fastened the seat belt.

Rosemary watched hesitantly for a minute, but when he closed the door she straightened her shoulders and circled the car to get in beside him. "All right," she announced firmly. "I'll drive, but if I make any mistakes you'd better not yell at me."

"I wouldn't dream of it," he said, and leaned his head against the seatback, closing his eyes.

"I should hope not," she said under her breath. She heard his gruff chuckle, but he didn't answer. When she didn't start the engine immediately he turned to open one eye. "Something else?" he asked.

They were about to take a giant step in their relationship, and he was so calm, while she was as nervous as a cat. Cat! She'd almost forgotten. "I have to stop at the cottage to feed the kitten. Do you mind?"

"Of course not."

THE DRIVE WAS SHORT, less than five miles, but by the time they arrived at the cottage Rosemary felt that her fingers were permanently fixed around the steering wheel. Yet she had made no major mistakes, at least none that Ryan, with his eyes closed, would have noticed. She was rather proud of herself.

Switching off the engine, she turned to smile her triumph at him. "I..." He had fallen asleep. Her eyes skidded across his beloved features. The wind dipping in through the open roof had rumpled his hair, and the moonlight streaked it silver. A shining lock fell forward over his broad forehead.

"He's asleep, Butch, out in the car," she told the cat a few minutes later as she scraped a part of a can of food into his bowl. "I'm sorry to leave you like this, but he really needs me tonight. He's so tired."

"Me-e-ek," the kitten answered, cocking his head as though he understood every word.

"I'll be late, so don't wait up. And don't worry about me even if I don't get home until morning."

"Me-eek."

She spread her hands and lifted her shoulders. "What can I say?" she answered with a grin.

RYAN WAS STILL SLEEPING when they reached his house. Quietly she released her seat belt and turned. Her hand brushed back the lock of hair and lingered. "Ryan," she whispered.

"Hmm." He stirred but didn't open his eyes.

She leaned closer, across the console, letting her knuckles stroke his cheek lightly. "Ryan, we're home."

Suddenly his eyes were open, their gray color almost obscured by the dilation of his pupils. He reached up to grasp her hand, holding it tightly to his cheek. "I want you more than I've ever wanted anything in my life."

"I want you, too, my darling." Her voice was strong and sure.

The mustache spread with his grin. "Then what the hell are we doing sitting here in a car?"

"You were the one who fell asleep!" There was no hurry now; they had all night, so she responded to his teasing tone. "And I want to tell you, Mr. Tarleton, that the idea of you falling asleep isn't very flattering. Ryan, maybe—"

"Don't say it," he interrupted. "Don't even think about leaving me tonight." He was out of the car by now, and the words were delivered through the opening in the sun roof.

"Ordering me around again, boss?" she said with an attempt at lightness. But her heart was jumping crazily in her chest as she slid the roof closed between them.

He leaned down to stick his head through the open door. "If I thought I could get away with it, I certainly would." He grinned as she got out and came around the car to join him.

Ryan handed her his jacket, picked up the suitcase and pulled her under his other arm. Lifting his gaze to the house, he breathed deeply, inhaling the freshness of the night air. "Ahh," he exhaled on a sigh. "It's really good to be home."

Rosemary slipped her arm around his waist and walked close to him as they mounted the steps. "Was it a bad trip?" she asked, looking up.

It struck her suddenly how domestic this scene was. She might have been his wife, waiting for him to come home, asking how his business had gone. Was that what she wanted? To belong to Ryan? To have the right to ask? Nonsense! The little woman waiting for her breadwinner to come home—that wasn't her at all. Besides, she could never live in a small town permanently. She would dry up and die without the stimulation of the city. It would be extremely foolish, not to mention dangerous, to let herself feel anything deeper than desire. That was strong enough!

Ryan stumbled slightly on the top step, lurching against her. He was staring, searching her eyes with an astonished gleam in his own.

"I'm sorry," she apologized quickly. "I had no right to pry into your business." She moved away from him.

"No, no," Ryan said, shaking his head slightly to clear it. Dear God! For a moment he had been struck by the domesticity of the scene. Rosie might have been his wife, asking about his business trip. "It wasn't that. I'm just tired."

For four years he'd called his feelings for this woman "infatuation" and "physical attraction." Now he wondered. For ten days she had never been very far from the surface of his mind, ready to spring to the forefront at the least loss of control. On more than one occasion he had found himself remembering the scent of her skin, the taste of her lips, instead of concentrating on the demands of the labor-union official across the table.

Ryan pulled himself up sharply as he opened the

front door and stood back to let her precede him into the house.

A dim light burned in the entrance hall, throwing her profile into sharp relief. His gaze dropped unbidden to the thrust of her breasts against the silken fabric of her blouse. He almost moaned aloud at the sight. Physical need was one thing. He wanted her with a hunger he hadn't experienced before, but the most foolhardy thing he could do would be to fall in love with Rosemary again. She was going through a bad time now, but she'd soon be over it. And when she was, she'd be ready to go home to New York, to resume her former life. She could never be content to settle down in a small town.

If he wasn't so tired he could think clearly. Pictures formed in his mind: Rosemary in a wedding gown, a gold band on her finger, Rosie with their child at her breast. "I need a shower!" he blurted out.

Her brows rose. "So? That sounds good to me...." She shrugged in a typical New Yorker's gesture, bringing a reluctant smile to his lips. She was a darling. He forgot his reservations in a rush of affection for her, moved by the sight of so much delicious feminity packed in such a slight body. His mouth was suddenly parched with the longing to drink from her moistness.

"Rosie, let's go upstairs." It would be all right. He was tired, but if he could just get upstairs he was sure everything would be all right. He returned her smile.

Rosemary's eyes fell under the blaze of his. Her heart took up the slow, heavy beat of arousal. Heat poured through her veins to warm every part of her body with expectancy. "I—" She had to clear her throat.

The stairs looked like a mountain to Ryan, but he determindedly put one foot in front of the other until the mountain was conquered. The long windows in his bedroom were undraped, so that the moonlight streamed in, providing enough brightness to see the hesitancy in Rosemary's expression. "Are you okay, honey?" he asked, turning her into his arms. He buried his face in the fragrant spill of her hair, inhaling slowly.

Her arms circled his waist. She arched against him, and he grasped her hips to bring her closer. Then a curse erupted from his throat, but Rosemary heard the desperation in his voice, as well, and something that sounded like a sob. With an electric jolt that shocked her, she felt the rather obvious evidence that his desire was waning. He didn't want her. This whole thing was a horrible mistake! Her eyes flooded with tears, blurring the shape of the bed. His physical rejection hurt worse than any pain she had ever had. She realized in the moment of loss that she loved Ryan, loved him with a depth of emotion she hadn't known she was capable of feeling. The knowledge almost robbed her lungs of air.

Her love expanded to save his pride. He couldn't help it if he'd mistaken his feelings for her, or that his feelings had changed so drastically. How could she get out of this with a semblance of dignity? She started to pull free of his arms, yet they only tightened around her. "Ryan, let me go," she demanded softly.

"No!"

"Ryan, I don't understand."

Finally he lifted his head to look down at her. She framed his face, studying carefully the pain and longing in his eyes, an emotional intensity that seemed to equal her own. Maybe he would never return her love, but he did want her. The relief that poured into her was overwhelming. What was wrong, though?

"Rosie, love. Sweetest Rosie." He raised a trembling hand to brush her tumbled hair away from her face. "The spirit is willing—hell, the spirit is desperate—but the flesh is weak."

Her jaw went slack; her eyes were as big as saucers.

A choking sound, almost a chuckle, came from his throat. "Lord, can you believe it?" he gasped, shaking his head.

She chuckled, too, but hers came out as more of a strangled puff of air. Then she giggled, and then released a full-throated laugh.

"It isn't funny!" Nevertheless he joined in helplessly, collapsing on the bed, pulling her with him. "Damn you, it isn't funny."

She wiped her streaming eyes and sat up in the middle of the mattress, trying to look sober. "You're right, it isn't funny," she said, and grabbed her stomach as she went into further peals of laughter. "Oh, Ryan!"

All at once he was under control. He frowned. "Well, it isn't *that* funny," he said, very much like a thwarted child.

"Oh, yes it is! Don't you see? We were tiptoeing around each other like two strangers trying to be polite, instead of like friends who have shared a lot." Rosemary had to stop for a calming breath. "We were trying so hard not to touch a sensitive spot—if you'll pardon the pun—and all the time it was totally unnecessary." She reached out to smooth his mustache. "I want you for my lover, but I also want to keep you as my friend," she murmured, smiling tentatively.

Ryan grinned reluctantly and turned his mouth into her palm. His lips played there on the soft skin. "Tonight would you settle for 'friend'?"

"I suppose I'll have to, won't I?" she teased.

His beautiful gray eyes moved tenderly over each of her features. "You're wonderful."

He hesitated, but she didn't speak, realizing there was more he wanted to say. She searched the smoky depths, surprised to find a hint of vulnerability, which was quickly hidden behind a noncommittal smile. That glimpse into his inner self touched something deep within her, some delicate emotion that blossomed, expanding her newfound love into a wish to protect, to succor, to cherish.

"I want to hold you," he said quietly. "Will you stay with me? Spend the night in my arms?"

"Yes," she said without hesitation. "Of course I will."

ROSEMARY SHIFTED RESTLESSLY under the restriction around her waist. She frowned in her sleep, then rolled over to bury her face in the pillow, but the movement brought no relief. Why was she sleeping in pajamas? She never slept in...

A deep, husky chuckle, a masculine chuckle, penetrated the brain-clouding fog like a ray of sunshine. Her head came up with a jerk. She was staring at an unfamiliar wall, six inches in front of her nose and painted a nauseating mustard color. Carefully and slowly she turned her head in the direction of the sound, peering through the black curtain of her hair.

Ryan sat on a chair beside the bed, his back to the window. The early light of dawn silhouetted his body, but she could see that his hair was damp and neatly combed, his mouth curved in an appealing grin, his hips covered insufficiently by a towel. His elbows rested on bare knees, and his fists held up his chin. How long had he been there? He looked amused, and clean and altogether male.

All those things registered in the space of the second it took Rosemary to press her face back into the pillow with a groan. "You look like a tiger about to devour its prey."

"I can't hear you," he said mildly. "Take the pillow out of your mouth."

She shook her head as the mattress beside her gave with his weight. His hand rested in the small of her back for a moment before moving up her spin to tangle in her hair. "Honey, please wake up." His voice was as hushed as a sigh and charming in its very quiet. He smoothed her hair away from her nape, leaving a fleeting kiss there. "I'm missing you."

She shivered, resisting the entreaty in his voice. "I have to brush my teeth."

The sweep of his mustache against her nape told her he was smiling. He placed his hands flat on the bed on each side of her shoulders. "Okay."

"I don't have a toothbrush."

"You can use mine." His breath was warm and moist on her neck.

"Hmm."

"Or, there's a spare in the guest bath," he went on as though she hadn't interrupted.

"May I have some coffee?" she persisted, not really understanding why she was being so contrary.

He drew back and was silent for a long minute. "Sweetheart, are you trying to pay me back for last night?"

"No!" She flipped over onto her back. Her eyes were wide as they met his skeptical look; her quick denial was genuine. She modified her tone. "I'm just not at my best in the morning."

He smiled tenderly and pushed her hair off her face. "Not even a little bit of revenge in your heart?"

"No...at least I don't think so," she acknowledged honestly. She would have liked to have been able to admit to him that she had had a great deal of trouble falling asleep last night. She had lain, watching him in the spill of moonlight, his breathing deep and regular, and felt her frustration grow with every breath. This morning, however, it wasn't so easy to confide that information. He was totally in control of himself, and she had lost the frustration, and those indulgent feelings.

His eyes narrowed. "You only want me when you have the upper hand," he said without expression.

She was horrified at the idea. It made her seem like an emasculator. "Oh, Lord, I hope not," she whispered with complete sincerity. "I don't know myself very well, but I pray I'm not like that."

Ryan pulled her forcefully into his arms in a brief hug of apology. Why had he said such a stupid thing? "Of course you're not like that, Rosie. I suppose I'm just trying to relieve my own embarrassment." Embarrassment, hah! Humiliation was more like it. He couldn't believe that any amount of exhaustion could have kept him from making love to her last night, when he had thought about nothing else for so long. Fighting the impatience that coursed through him now to make up for the loss, he straightened and stood up, reaching for her hand. "Come on. I'll find you a toothbrush."

She slid out of bed, stumbling slightly on the hems of the pajamas that puddled around her feet.

Ryan knelt immediately to roll the legs up for her. His long fingers curled around her ankle like a warm bracelet. "Where on earth did you find these?" he asked, tilting his face up to smile at her, hoping the light words would distract her from his trembling hands.

She balanced with a hand on his shoulder and extended the other foot. "I rooted through your drawers. I hope you don't mind."

"Not a bit. I'm glad you found something. I presume I was a lousy host. I'm afraid I don't remember much after my, er, failure."

Her other hand rested lightly on his bent head. "You were exhausted," she murmured softly. Her voice dropped to the merest whisper. "It upset me to see you like that."

With a playful growl Ryan stood and swung her into his arms. Her sweet lips, parted in astonishment, were a lure he struggled to resist. If he kissed her now there would be no stopping him. He strode out the door and down the hall to the guest bath, where he deposited a bemused Rosemary on her feet.

The cabinet under the sink yielded a new toothbrush and a tube of toothpaste. He dug around further to come up with a hairbrush, comb, scented soap and bath beads, all still in their original packaging. He dumped everything into her hands with a rueful grin. "Hurry, love," he said huskily.

Even the coffee maker was against him, he mourned silently. Though it gurgled and choked, making a great deal of racket, each drop seemed to cling for eternal moments before it fell into the glass pot below.

He was coming up the stairs carrying a tray when Rosemary emerged from the bathroom. "Mmm, coffee," she said. "Thank you, darling."

The words might be commonplace, but her smile was like none he'd ever seen her wear, knowing and intimate, a smile that named her Helen, Cleopatra, Juliet, a smile that men would kill for in ancient times. And he could understand the motivation that had driven them to it. He almost fell literally at her feet.

She had disposed of the oversized pajama bottoms, and the pajama top left a lot of bare, beautiful leg showing. Her hair spilled across her shoulders, curving and waving, madly shimmering in blue-black exhilaration. Her face was free of makeup, but had been scrubbed until her skin was pink and glowing.

Numbly he followed her into the bedroom; he stood there holding the tray and staring at her like a fool. She turned back, took the tray from his lifeless hands and, bending gracefully, deposited it on the floor. When she stood up, she rose all the way to her tiptoes and slid her arms around his neck.

"Is something wrong, Ryan?" she asked innocently. The expression in her eyes was far from innocent. She was a woman at her most seductive, in men's clothing, sexy and feminine as hell, and smelling like heaven. Her scent was hot summer garden roses, heady and alluring, and acted on him like a powerful aphrodisiac.

Ryan's arms came around her convulsively; blindly he searched for her lips. They were parted and waiting. She tasted exquisite, sweet and fresh. Her mouth was warm, slick with moisture, delicious to his roving, exploring tongue. He heard a moan and wondered if it had come from himself.

Rosemary marveled at Ryan's racing heartbeat. She could feel the vibration through the soft cotton of the pajamas she wore, through her skin and nerves and muscle, until that life-giving tempo seemed to merge with her own vital rhythm somewhere deep within her, somewhere so deep that it might have been the home of her soul. The rhythm of his heart was picked up by her heated blood, carrying it through her body until her entire being melted with this feeling of oneness that was love.

When Ryan raised his head he was breathing as though his lungs were starved for air. His eyes had a glazed, unfocused look, and his voice was a raw, hoarse murmur. "Rosie. Beautiful, glorious Rosie." He sought the soft skin of her neck with his moist lips, pushing the collar out of the way in his quest.

She felt the sensual brush of his mustache at her throat, behind her ear, at her nape, as she buried her hands in his thick hair. Her slender frame moved of its own accord, arching, fitting itself to him.

She heard herself whimper, protesting when she realized he was pushing her away, until she felt his hands at the buttons of the pajama top. There were only three. She was grateful for that, and he made short work of them. But when she would have shrugged out of it he kept the sides together in his trembling fists.

"Slowly, darling. Or I may be more of a disappointment to you this morning than I was last night."

Her gaze met his.

"You've set me on fire, sweetheart. I'm about to go up in flames. Give me a minute." His smile was weak, half-derisive, half-hungry. "I want our first time together to be perfect."

"Ryan, please hold me."

Releasing one handful of fabric, he grazed her cheek with his fingers as he lifted his hand to smooth her hair away from her temple. His lips played over the exposed spot. "We're going to do this right if it kills me," he grated. His other hand held her shoulder in a tender grip. "And it just may. After last night...my desire for you is close to the explosion point."

Rosemary had never experienced such intensely heightened emotions. They shook her to the core, were almost too much, and she knew Ryan saw that. She subsided against him, content to let him lead.

His arms took her weight, his hands stroking lightly down her back, their touch firm and reassuring, and she found her face pressed gently into the warmth of his throat. She nuzzled closer, much like a young kitten seeking comfort.

Ryan laughed softly. "You're a delightful contradiction, love," he said into her ear. "One minute you're a seductive sophisticate, and the next an endearing waif."

"And you. Last night you aroused all my sympathetic instincts, and this morning I'm wondering why," she told him with a hint of annoyance in her voice. The annoyance wasn't directed at him but at herself. She wasn't sure about these fluctuating emotions.

He drew back and lifted a brow, whether from her words or her tone she didn't know. "You seem hesitant, Rosie, but I don't understand why. You're not innocent," he said quietly.

"No, but I've...dammit, Ryan. I'm not that experienced, and you're rather overwhelming, you know." She wasn't about to add that she had fallen head over heels in love with him. He wouldn't welcome such a confession.

Very carefully he framed her face in his hands. "You've got that backward," he said ruefully. "But, honey, I don't want to overwhelm you. I want us to share."

His smile was like a gift, and she responded unhesitatingly. "I'd like that."

This time when his mouth touched hers it was

infinitely tender, his lips moving across from corner to corner with little nips, his tongue teasing rather than penetrating the line of her mouth. The sensation was even more erotic than his first, unrestrained kiss. His breath invaded her senses, intoxicating her as thoroughly as the finest brandy.

If he wanted them to share, this was not the right way to go about it, thought Rosemary vaguely. He was liable to find her like a pool of warm jello at his feet. She swayed. Only the large hands at her shoulders kept her from dropping as though she'd been pole-axed. "You do this too well," she said weakly. "Prop me up somewhere."

"I have a better idea." He lifted her unresisting body and crossed to the bed.

"Oh, yes. This is much better," she breathed as he placed her in the middle of the mattress among the tumbled sheets.

He discarded his towel and lay beside her, not touching but only a short space away. Drawn like a magnet to his magnificent body, she put out a hand toward his hair-roughened chest, but he caught her wrist and brought it to his lips. "Me first," he said huskily. His hand slid under the fabric of the pajama top to cup her breast. As she watched in fascination his lids drooped heavily for a minute. When they lifted again the fire he had said she'd lit was burning free, and in another minute had rekindled in her.

His fingers were doing magic things, stroking over her swelling flesh, lightly, then spreading to cover her completely. "Ryan!" She stretched into his caress, needing, craving, wordlessly demanding a firmer touch.

He eased her onto her back and finally pushed aside the shirt. Motionless, his eyes wide with wonder, he simply looked at her for a long minute. Then his hands swept her length, from shoulders to ankles and back. "This is why," he murmured enigmatically. "I've never known a woman to be so desirable, so tantalizing." His lips began to follow the same trail his hands had taken, slowly, leisurely, until she was mindless beneath him.

Rosemary plunged her fingers into his hair. "Ryan, please," she entreated, using her hands to urge him into the vicinity of her lips. Then she was covering him with kisses, murmuring husky phrases, stretching luxuriously toward his arousal.

Gently he opened her legs, and sank with a single stroke into the waiting source of her femininity. With a slight, hungry little shift, the cradle of her hips welcomed him, and they were together as though they'd been designed to harmonize only with each other, only this man, only this woman, in the entire universe.

"Oh, sweet—" His breath caught on the last of the endearment. Lips covering hers in a moment of exquisite reverence, his hips began to move with erotic grace. He ignited such flames in her, in himself, that the crescendo, when it came, was simultaneous and total, a rhythmic duet that stole the power of speech. He held her securely, and she clung to him with complete trust that they would reach the moment of climactic ecstacy.

Finally, when her soft cry was but an echo in her memory, when his breathing had calmed enough, he rolled to the side, keeping her body in his protective embrace.

His touch was gentle as he caressed her from the delicate bones of her shoulder to the ripe curve of her hip. For a long time they were quiet, content, almost dozing. The light in the room, filtering through the curtains, warmed subtly from the cool blue of dawn to the pale gold of morning. A dreaminess wrapped around her like a down comforter.

"Even the five-year wait was worth it," Ryan whispered into her hair.

"I'm glad," she answered softly. "It was for me, too." Her fingers found and massaged the back of his neck. The action brought her breasts into contact with his chest, her eyes into contact with his. She could only survive that look for a moment. She laid her cheek against his heart, loving the sound beneath her ear.

He sighed deeply. "But I don't want to conduct a long-distance affair, Rosie. You in New York, me here."

"That would probably be very frustrating," she agreed with a small smile.

He shifted slightly, and she tilted her head back to look into his eyes. "Something's bothering you," she said with a perception born of love.

"Uh-huh. I'm wide open to you again, and it scares the hell out of me."

"Ryan, I wouldn't..."

His expression stopped the rest of the statement. "Don't make promises you can't keep," he told her almost harshly. "I managed to survive your leaving me once. I'm not sure I could handle it today."

And you'll never leave Apple Valley. Living in the city would kill you, she thought silently, remembering the pride and complete contentment in his voice whenever he spoke of the farm. She didn't want to be responsible for what he would become if he were taken out of his beloved Georgia. Ryan was the type to visit the city occasionally for a change of scene, but not to live there permanently. The life would smother and suffocate all the things that made Ryan the man he was.

That left one alternative. And that was even more inconceivable.

Just then Ryan lifted her chin with his strong fingers and looked long and deeply into her eyes. She knew what he saw there would confirm his fears. Rosemary could never be content to make her home here.

"I could try," she said suddenly. "You never know until you try something whether or not it will work. And we're not talking about something permanent." *Are we,* she added silently, waiting, wanting him to dispute her words, not wanting it. But anticipation had already been seeded by her love, and before she realized what was happening, that hope began to bloom.

Rosemary knew that love alone was often not enough to sustain a relationship. She had seen devoted couples destroy themselves, and each other in the process, by trying to be what their partners wanted, even if that wasn't what they wanted themselves. She and Ryan would have to be honest. "I want to know the things you like, Ryan. I want to really know the man you are here. It might not work, but would we ever be able to forgive ourselves if we didn't investigate the possibility?"

He opened his mouth to speak, but she stopped the words with her fingers. "Don't say anything right now. Don't say a word. We could try, couldn't we? Couldn't you share your kind of life with me while I'm here?" When he didn't answer she felt the disappointment clear to her toes, until she realized she still had his mouth covered. "Nod if you think I'm right," she ordered beguilingly.

Instead of the nod she was engulfed in a huge hug, reinforced with laughter. "Oh, sweetheart! Yes, we could try. I don't know whether it will work, but we can give ourselves time to try."

Ryan sobered as his head fell back onto the pillow. He was on guard, afraid to let his feelings mellow. There was no way Rosemary Addison would ever be content to live for the rest of her life in Apple Valley. She might think she could, but he knew her; he refused to even acknowledge the possibility. Why else was she qualifying her commitment with phrases like "while I'm here"? The exhaustion that had plagued him yesterday returned unexpectedly.

While in England he had visited his sister and brother-in-law. Their blatant pride in their new son, his mother's delight in her first grandson, had made him realize what he had missed in life. And though he tried not to blame it on Rosemary, he couldn't help but think of what might have been.

"What is it, Ryan?" she asked, her worried glance letting him know she had picked up on his sudden restraint.

He glanced down at her face, her cheek resting on his chest, and forced himself to smile. "Nothing, Rosie. Nothing, I promise you."

"But you looked so earnest," she protested.

He chuckled. Earnest. That was as good a word as any. Earnest, scared, afraid of loving her, afraid of losing her. It would be all right, he cautioned himself, if he didn't fall too deeply in love. That would be disastrous. All at once his mood grew playful. He could bear up under the strain of having this delectable woman in his bed, in his life; he could bear up very well.

"I was. Earnestly contemplating your delectable body," he said with a grin. He rose enough to tumble her off his chest and onto her back. Planting his hands on either side of her shoulders, he loomed over her, leering with his best villain imitation, hoping she would be distracted. Instead he found the distraction was on his side.

His gaze was drawn to her breasts, captivated by the sight of the rosy peaks as they changed shape, stiffening in response, not to a touch, but merely to his attentive regard. They seemed to be reaching up to him in anticipation.

"Earnestly contemplating further ravishment of your beautiful body," he amended as he lowered his head to touch one nipple lightly with his tongue. It responded immediately, tightening more. "Damn, that's fascinating." He bathed the other and watched it echo the sweet pleading of its mate.

Rosemary's breathing was becoming erratic under the tender assault. "Ryan," she protested weakly.

Thoughtfully he lifted his head to look at her.

She waited.

"I just want to play with this amazing new toy," he said with an innocent grin.

"You devil!" She laughed. "I should have known you'd say something outrageous."

"Oh! If it's 'outrageous' you want, I have a whole repertoire of 'outrageous.' Like—"

She pulled his head down to seal his lips.

BREAKFAST WAS AN HILARIOUS AFFAIR. Ryan cooked—if his effort could be called that. He took bacon and waffles from the freezer and put them in the microwave.

"Where's Zack?" Rosemary asked.

"He and his wife come on Monday and Friday. She cleans, and he keeps the freezer stocked. The Sunday you arrived was a special occasion."

"I'm honored. Aren't we having grits?" She peered around him to watch as he thawed frozen orange juice under the hot-water tap.

"You don't serve grits with waffles. Even a Yankee ought to know that. Too much starch." He stripped off the white seal and flipped open the can with his thumb. He smiled down at her, wrapped securely in his oversized robe. "Did you like the grits?" He dumped the thick orange nectar into a waiting pitcher and swiveled the faucet to the cold-water side.

"They weren't too bad," she answered casually under the satisfied gleam in his eyes.

"Weren't bad? I'll have you know grits is considered Southern ice cream." He frowned. "Grits are..." He shrugged. "I never could get the verb right."

"You're in a good mood this morning," she observed. Ducking her head, she slid in under his arm, greatly hampering his activity at the sink, but he didn't seem to mind.

In between filling the can with cold water he nuzzled the side of her neck. "Yes, I am," he said quietly against her skin. "Are you?"

"The best. What are we going to do today?"

He reached around her to turn off the tap. "What would you like to do?"

She twisted in his arms until her back was to the sink and she was looking up at him. "Whatever you would normally do on a Saturday at home," she answered. At his dubious expression she went on. "I mean it, Ryan. I want to enjoy the things you enjoy."

"Okay. We'll drive down to Atlanta for the Braves game."

"Good. What time does it start?"

"At two. We can stay for dinner and still be back here in time for an early night."

"Together."

"Definitely together."

"And then what can we do tomorrow?"

He grinned. "Whoa. Why don't we let tomorrow take care of itself?"

"No, Ryan. I want to get a good start on learning the things you like."

His hips moved suggestively against hers. "I like this," he growled from deep in his throat.

"I know you like that, but I want to do something *else* you like." She wiggled to be free.

Reluctantly he let her go. "Well, let's see." He picked up the pitcher and poured juice into glasses. "We could go rafting on the river."

"That sounds like fun. What do we have to do?"

"Not much. Drag out the rafts, inflate them, toss them into the back of the truck and drive to the river. We'll have to take two cars and leave one where we'll come out." He snapped his fingers. "And we should take Carole with us. She loves rafting."

Rosemary hadn't been thinking of sharing their day with anyone else, but she liked Carole. Why not?

Rosemary was determined to give it her best shot. She shared Ryan's reservations about this whole scene—she could be hurt very deeply if they grew too close—but she had never been one to back down from a challenge. And this challenge promised to be worth the gamble.

THE GAME WENT into extra innings and dinner turned out to be hot dogs and beer, which suited Rosemary fine—except that the beer made her sleepy. By the time the Atlanta Braves finally put away the San Diego Padres in the twelfth, she was nodding off against Ryan's shoulder.

He gave a tug to the sun visor he'd bought to protect her face. "Hey, sleepyhead, wake up. It's time to go home."

"I'm not asleep," she protested. "Just resting my eyes." They got to their feet with several thousand others and made their way slowly to the gate. Well, at least the baseball season only went on for a couple of months. Didn't it? It wasn't that she hadn't had a good time at the game, she told herself sternly. It had just gone on so *long*. And it was so hot sitting out in the sun.

She was glad Ryan had insisted she wear the jacket that matched her light-blue cotton sun dress; her shoulders would really have been burned if he hadn't thought of it. As it was, the short sleeves had left her forearms bare, and they were stinging uncomfortably.

Ryan's arm slid protectively around her waist to

keep her next to him in the crowd. She forgot all about the discomfort as she smiled up at him. "That was fun," she murmured, letting her cheek rest on the smooth material of his yellow knit sport shirt.

"Did you really enjoy it?" he asked with a distinctly doubtful smile.

"Yes, I did," she lied. Well, it wasn't *exactly* a lie.

9

"RYAN! LOOK AT ME," Rosemary grumbled.

Ryan stuck his head out of the bathroom door. He was naked to the waist, and shaving cream clung to his cheeks except for one path down the right side of his face. "What is it, honey?"

Wordlessly she held out her arms. Without the jacket the contrast between the pale skin of her upper arms and the bright red of her forearms was startling.

"Oh, love, I'm sorry. Does it hurt badly? I'll get something to put on it." He started to turn back to the bathroom.

"The burn doesn't hurt at all. Or hardly at all. But look at me. I look like a clown. I'll have to wear long sleeves for a week."

The razor in his hand dripped a blob of shaving cream onto the carpet as he stood staring at her speechlessly.

She realized her mistake almost at once. She was sounding like a spoiled child. What difference did a little sunburn make? She would have to overcome this tendency to exaggerate things that were of no importance. "It doesn't matter, I guess," she conceded.

"I can see how it would if you were planning to wear a designer gown to the opera tonight," he conceded dryly.

"You're right, of course." She let her arms drop disconsolately to her sides.

The ironic expression disappeared from Ryan's face at once, to be replaced by tender understanding. He came over to where she stood in front of the mirror and folded her in his arms, ignoring the shaving cream. "You have a little ways to go, Rosie. After all, you've been conditioned for twenty-nine years to the importance of certain things."

"Things that are really very unimportant," she agreed, rubbing her cheek against his, smearing herself with shaving cream. She liked the smell.

"I didn't say that."

"No, but you implied it, and you're right." With both hands she cradled his face, covering his ears. "And make that almost thirty years."

He shook his head in resignation and chuckled, entering into the game. With a finger he traced a white, soapy line across the bridge of her nose, over her cheek, into her hairline. "Is your age still bothering you?" he asked, leaning away to inspect his work.

"No." Carefully she removed a dab of cream from his mustache and wrote an 'R' on his brow.

He glanced in the mirror behind her shoulder. "Are you branding me, woman?" Abandoning the game for more interesting pleasures, his hands found the zipper of her sun dress and lowered it.

Rosemary stepped away, letting the garment fall

to her feet, then went to work on his trousers. "Yes, do you mind?" she asked playfully when they stood face to face, he in his briefs, she in her panties and strapless bra, both their faces smeared white.

"Hell, no. Be my guest." He scooped her up in his arms and headed back for the bathroom. He turned on the shower spray, urging her into the stall. Quickly he stepped out of his briefs and joined her. "Now what were we talking about?" he asked, watching avidly as she stripped to bare skin. The water had already cleaned her face of shaving cream, carrying it in tiny rivulets down her body. He put out a finger to catch a dribble that clung to the tip of her shiny, wet breast.

"Nothing important at all," she said, raising her two-toned arms to encircle his neck.

He laughed against her mouth. "You catch on fast...." His hands cupped her bottom, pulling her closer to his arousal. "Speaking of which, you ever made love in a shower?"

"No," she said in a voice husky with both amusement and desire. "And I don't think it will work. You're too tall."

"It'll work," he promised. "All you have to do is put your leg...no, like this...."

"Ry-an."

"It'll work, Rosie. Trust me."

And it did.

LATER AS SHE LAY with her head pillowed on his chest, she made a face at the mustard color on the wall. "Do you still want me to do something about this house?"

"Mmm, when you have time."

"Who on earth picked out the paint?"

Ryan opened his eyes to follow the direction of her gaze. "The painter," he said lazily. "I didn't have time to fool with picking out colors. I figured that was his job." He eased her gently off where she lay sprawled across his chest and rolled to his side to face her, only inches away. "I used to hate the color, but for the past couple of days I've hardly noticed."

"Mustard is fine on a hot dog, but it's rather strong for a bedroom with Southern exposure." She tangled her fingers in his hair, ruffling it slightly before tugging his head closer for a gentle kiss.

His hand slid slowly down her side, pausing briefly at the dip in her waist before circling around to squeeze her derriere. "Speaking of Southern exposure..."

"Keep your mind on decor for a minute, buster. I have a huge antique tester bed in storage that would look beautiful in here. The lines are very masculine, and—"

"No," he said flatly. "I told you, Rosemary, that you weren't to put any of your furniture in this house."

She was surprised at the fierce tone but tried not to let her reaction show. Why was he so adamant? The furniture was just sitting there, not doing anyone any good. "Okay. It was just a thought."

"You can think about the house later," he informed her in a softer, more seductive voice as his wandering hand stroked down her thigh and back up to tease the warm center of her feminity. "Can't you?"

"Yes. Oh, yes...Ryan."

ROSEMARY LOOKED over her shoulder to make sure she couldn't be heard. Carole and her boyfriend, Andy, were unloading the paddles from the pickup. "This could really be interesting if we were alone," she told Ryan in an undertone as he knelt in front of her, arranging the strap of a life preserver between her legs. She was wearing a black maillot with one of Ryan's white shirts, knotted at the waist.

"Hush, brat," he scolded with a gleam in his eyes that told her she was right. His hand lingered for a moment at the back of her knee.

"You're so inventive that I'll bet we could—"

His laugher muffled the rest of her words. He rose, giving her a swat on the fanny. "Hop in," he said, holding the inflated rubber raft steady.

"Carole? Andy? You ready?" he called.

"Sure," the young blonde answered. "Did you get the cooler?"

"Already loaded."

Carole hopped into the second of the two-man rafts without aid, Rosemary noticed. She noticed something else, as well. Carole was definitely smitten with her boss, and Ryan didn't even know it. But Andy did. The poor young man wore his expression of misery like a hair shirt. It was obvious he was Carole's devoted if unnoticed slave. Carole treated him more like a brother.

This promises to be a ludicrous afternoon, thought Rosemary. *Andy loves Carole. Carole loves Ryan. And who does Ryan love? Rosemary? No, Ryan doesn't love anyone—yet.* She hoped to change that situation. In the meantime she decided to be especially nice to Andy.

The river was placid as they pushed off and not very wide at that point. The branches of great oaks met across the width to form a green canopy. The rafts bumped together lazily as the river took them along on its current.

Rosemary grabbed a paddle, beginning to row eagerly, until Ryan ordered her to sit back and relax. The river would do the work. The paddles were for steering, he informed her, and her efforts were threatening to beach them on the bank. "We don't want to end up in the mud again, do we, honey?"

Carole heard the remark and laughed lightly. "Rosemary told me about her first driving lesson, Ryan. I found her to be a very able student."

"I broke her in for you," Ryan teased back. "Did you see the game on TV yesterday?"

"Wonderful game," Carole agreed, with too much enthusiasm, in Rosemary's opinion. "I can't think of anyone I'd rather beat than the Padres."

Despite herself Rosemary felt a stab of jealousy at

their easy camaraderie. She had to keep reminding herself that she really liked Carole.

She had her back to the pointed bow of the raft, enjoying the luxury of watching Ryan in cutoff jeans and sneakers and a gray shirt exactly the color of his eyes. The ripple of muscle where the ribbed-knit sleeve circled his biceps, the strength in his hands as he maneuvered the single paddle at the back of the raft with easy competence, the long muscles of his thighs, his calves—she sighed. He was all man, and it was hard to blame any woman for being attracted to him.

Her eyes lifted from their study of his body to meet his amused gaze. He knew exactly what she was thinking, and he was thoroughly enjoying himself. She smiled back, then let her eyelids fall half-shut, teasing him with suggestive glances from beneath her lashes. Their laughter mingled in the clear, pure air. Ryan leaned forward, his hand outstretched, and she put hers into it, responding to the warm pressure of his fingers. Words weren't necessary to express the pleasure they felt in each other's company.

Her first clue that the languid, peaceful voyage wasn't all there was to rafting came when a spray of river water drenched the arm she had draped gracefully over the bolsterlike side of the boat.

"How about opening me a beer, honey? Before we get to the rapids."

"Rapids?" Rosemary had sudden visions of huge boulders springing up from the middle of the river, ready and eager to rip into the fragile material of the raft. "As in boulders? Rushing water? Roller coaster?" She scrambled on her knees to the middle of the raft, where the cooler had been stowed, and opened the lid to pluck out two frosty cans.

"Not that bad. The Coosa is a trickle compared to the Colorado. More like a merry-go-round."

She sat back on her heels to open a beer and handed it to him. Just as she pulled the tab on the second can the raft gave a lurch; a few ounces of beer went down the front of her bathing suit. Ryan laughed at her expression.

That's your second clue, Rosemary, she thought, frowning. "I thought we'd just float along."

"Honey, I wouldn't have brought you if it was dangerous. The rapids are the fun part of the trip, and you're the one who wanted to come."

He was right. She had thought up the whole idea to begin with, had wanted to learn to do the things he liked. She plastered a smile on her face. "I know, Ryan. I'm sure it will be great!"

THREE HOURS LATER she felt the smile had been wiped away forever. She was soaked to the skin and shivering when she dragged herself into the cottage, waving a hand when Ryan touched the horn as he drove away. She felt bruised and battered from the tips of her toes to the top of her head.

Ryan had cheerfully told her that she'd done very well for the first time—she shuddered at the thought that there might be a second—and had left her with instructions to take a hot bath and she'd feel fine. He was coming back for dinner. She had muttered something about peanut butter, and he'd laughed again.

Honestly, she'd never heard so much laughter in her entire life. They had all laughed—Carole, Andy, Ryan—as if the trip had been a wonderful experience, rather than the torture she considered it. Yet she had played along. If her own laughter had been strained she was sure they hadn't noticed.

Rosemary wanted to be with Ryan. That was what she had to keep remembering, and these athletics were worth it to get to know him better, to see him in all sorts of settings. After all, this was temporary, an experience of the moment. She wasn't here forever, she told herself.

She turned on the water, seasoned it with violets and sank gratefully into the steaming water, lifting her hair to let it trail over the edge of the tub. "Ahh," she sighed.

"Me-ek…"

Opening one eye, she watched the kitten slide around the door. "Hello, Butch. You may come in, but you must be quiet. I'm dying, and I'd like to do it in peace."

The kitten ignored her complaining and began to investigate the room. He sniffed in every corner but evidently finding nothing that interested him, curled up in a black ball on one of the golden rugs.

Rosemary closed her eye again. She fell asleep almost instantly.

When she awoke a short while later, Ryan was standing beside the tub, a bathsheet in his hands and a strange expression in his eyes. The late-afternoon sunlight streamed in through the stained glass, painting his jeans and white shirt in all the rich colors of a potentate's robe.

She smiled sleepily. "Hi. Am I late, or are you early?"

"I'm a little early," he said quietly. "Come on out of there."

She started to rise, but her muscles refused to co-operate. "Ouch. I'm stiff." She groaned. "Can you give me a hand, please?"

Instead of a hand Ryan tossed the towel aside and reached into the tub to pick her up bodily. He held her close for a long minute, looking down at her hair, spilling across his arm like a sweet-smelling midnight cloud.

"Where's Butch?"

"He just scurried into the living room, and if he knows what's good for him, he'll stay away for a while."

Rosemary snuggled against his broad chest. Several buttons of the white shirt were open, and she couldn't resist the urge to slide her hand inside to touch the hair-roughened skin. "Your clothes are going to be wet," she warned, still in that sleepy voice.

"I'll take them off."

"Good." She sought the pulse point in his throat with her lips.

Setting her on her feet, Ryan reached for the towel. Very gently he blotted all the moisture from her skin.

Rosemary stood quietly under his ministrations, still caught up in the lethargy the hot bath had induced. The minor detail of her nudity didn't even occur to her. It felt good to be cared for like this, but the experience wasn't sensuous, she noted with some surprise. Here was Ryan touching her tenderly and intimately, making her feel infinitely comforted, not aroused.

When he'd finished he swung her up in his arms and headed for the bedroom. He placed her on the quilted coverlet and disappeared into the bath again. When he returned he had a bottle of the violet-scented lotion she'd used before. He had unbuttoned his shirt and pulled it loose from the waist of his jeans, baring all that tempting skin.

"Am I going to get a massage?" she asked, stretching luxuriously. The action lifted her breasts, and she watched his lips part slightly.

"Not if you don't stop that," he said with a sexy smile. "I should have realized you'd be stiff after all that physical exertion. Roll over."

She complied, folding her hands under her cheek with a contented sigh. He braced himself on one knee beside her hip and leaned forward. His large hands were warm and careful as he stroked and squeezed the strain from her muscles. Her nape, her shoulders and arms, her spine, her thighs and calves—all came under his careful touch. Places that she hadn't known were tense, like the soles of her feet and her fingertips, were treated to his loving attention.

Just when she thought there wasn't a bone in her body with any substance remaining, the tempo of the massage began to change subtly. The long fingers, which had pressed upward on her spine, veered out to brush the sides of her breasts with a featherlike touch. The sensation brought her awake instantly. And when she felt the soft whisk of his mustache at the dip in her back she caught her breath in an audible gasp.

"I thought you were asleep." The deep-voiced words were spoken against her backbone, then carried on sensitive nerve endings throughout her body, setting up a warm thrill of excitement.

"I thought I was, too," she murmured weakly. "But I don't think I am anymore."

His quiet laughter had the same effect as his words, following along the same nerve path. The thrill became a throb, and she started to move restlessly under his hands. He wasn't ready for her to turn, not yet.

Ryan's large hands slid underneath her to cup her breasts. She felt her already stiff nipples thrust hungrily into the center of his palms. He squeezed lightly and rotated his palms in a circular pattern so erotic that it threatened to send her over the edge of sanity. Leaning forward, he moved his torso carefully, side to side, against the skin of her back, using the hair on his chest as an instrument of tactile stimulation. Nuzzling her own hair aside, he added the provocation of his lips at her nape, nipping, tasting....

As though she needed more provocation! Rosemary moaned, twisting. "Ryan, please. I need you now...." Suddenly she was lifted, turned, her arms reaching for him. Her hands found their way into the loose collar of his shirt, and she scraped her nails over his shoulders and down, pulling him closer, trying to rid him of the garment.

He gasped, and his breathing accelerated just before his mouth came down to cover hers. She met his kiss frantically, her tongue joining the rough velvet of his in a sensual duel. Then she was pushing him away with a force that disturbed him, until he realized her hands were also pushing at the shirt clinging to his upper arms, moving down to grope for the snap of his jeans.

The shirt fell to the floor as he stood. His eyes never leaving hers, he stripped, jeans, briefs, shoes, in one swift motion. And then he was between her thighs, over her, a superb male animal. His hands tenderly sought her warmth, assuring himself that she was ready for him before he thrust his hips forward, penetrating the warm, moist cavern while an incoherent cry escaped him.

She received him eagerly, readily, with her arms, her mouth, her body, in wanton expectation and excitement. His name was a litany on her lips, repeated over and over, in rhythm with the movement of their bodies, the building, swelling tension, his name ending on a joyous sob at the moment of turbulent release.

His arms bound her, one hand under her hips lifting her to the momentum of his driving, convulsive climax. He cried out against the soft skin of her throat, and his body collapsed in helpless abandon.

"Lord, love," he rasped when he could speak. "I've never known anyone like you. You're wonderful."

Tears of joy and happiness pooled behind her lowered lids. "So are you," she whispered, clinging to him when he would have moved, not wanting to lose any of his magnificent weight. "Oh, so are you, my darling."

"I'm too heavy for you," he protested shakily, lifting his head. "Rosie! Oh, love," he crooned, stroking her damp hair away from her face. "Why are you crying? Did I hurt you?"

She opened her eyes to see his confusion and worry through the blur of tears. Her fingers slid into the thickness of his hair, the heels of her hands covering his ears. She smiled and moved his head between her hands in a little shake. "No. You could never hurt me."

She tried to lighten the supercharged moment with a frivolous explanation. "It's called weeping for joy." But her attempt fell flat, because the love that filled her heart to overflowing was anything but lighthearted. Her smile faded, giving her eyes a liquid radiance more eloquent than any declaration. Her trembling fingers swept across his mouth and back again to smooth the mustache. "You make me feel so good," she added in the barest whisper.

He dipped his head, his lips finding hers in a tender, butterfly-light kiss. When he raised his head the smile curving his sensual mouth was itself like an embrace, enchanting her. "Then I should be weeping, too," he murmured adoringly. "Because I feel fantastic."

Keeping her in his arms, he rolled to his side. Their faces were only inches apart. She inhaled the scent of his warm breath and searched his contented expression for a moment, wondering if she was about to make one of the biggest mistakes of her life. "Ryan, may I tell you something?" she asked softly.

He ran an affectionate finger down the length of her nose. "Of course you may."

"I think I'm falling in love with you." The words were a bald-faced lie. She didn't think; she knew she loved him, deeply and forever. But she also knew that she had a snowball in hell's chance of convincing him.

A shutter seemed to come down over those smoky gray eyes, and Rosemary felt like weeping again. She sensed his withdrawal even though he didn't loosen his loving embrace by an inch.

"So what does that mean, Rosie?" Ryan's voice was rough with doubt. "What do you want me to say?" Surely she wasn't ready to stay in Apple

Valley permanently. Or did she only mean she needed warmth and affection in her life? Being Rosemary, she wouldn't take without giving in return. But his doubts were still with him. At times he wished he *could* loosen his feelings, give her everything of himself that she seemed to need. But self-protection was too deeply ingrained.

Her eyes flooded with real tears; they rolled down to wet Ryan's shoulder under her cheek. He felt them before he saw them and gently wiped the moisture away with a thumb. "Please, don't," he said gruffly.

Men didn't like tears, a well-known fact borne out by Rosemary's own father. He had hated emotional reactions of any kind, had always preached control. Suddenly she realized she had felt more real emotion since leaving New York than she'd felt in her whole life before that. Fear, anger, even a little jealousy—love, passion, joy, and now maybe heartbreak.

Rosemary sniffed, squelching the tears through sheer willpower, and moved away from the comfort of his body. He let her go but half raised himself, propping his head in his hand to look down at her.

She lay flat on her back and spoke to the ceiling. "How do you know I would leave?"

"Do you expect me to believe you wouldn't? No, you'd have your apartment on Fifth Avenue, while I'd have the farm here. I don't believe any love would be strong enough to survive the obstacle of constant separation, and you'd never be content to live the rest of your life in Apple Valley, Georgia."

"I don't know, do I, until I try?" she answered boldly.

With a heavy sigh he dropped his head to the mattress. Rolling onto his back, he put his hands beneath his head. "Try? What do you have in mind, an experiment in alternate life-styles? I don't want you to experiment with me, Rosie."

"Ryan, I would never do that," she whispered, horrified that he could think such a thing. She stared at his unrelenting profile. "I'm not suggesting a sudden, rash decision. All I'm asking for is a chance to see if things could work between us."

A muscle in his jaw clenched, then relaxed. "The best thing we could ever have is what we have now. A relationship based on strong friendship and desire," he said firmly, obviously trying to convince himself as much as her.

The words sliced through Rosemary like a hot knife, leaving an unseen wound deep inside. She was fighting, too. Fighting for her happiness. "Okay!" she snapped. With a jerk she sat up, wrapping her arms around her knees, and looked over her shoulder at his guarded expression. She couldn't bear to see skepticism in his eyes, so she faced forward again. "Okay," she went on in a milder tone. "But don't shut me out without a chance. You're much more cosmopolitan than I am, Ryan."

He mumbled a protest, and she waved him to silence. "At least according to my definition. You're at home in any situation. You can fit in equally well in New York or here. I want to be able to do that, too. It's not an experiment I'm proposing—maybe it was before, a test for myself, but now I need a chance to adjust." When he didn't answer, she finally turned to him.

His expression clearly reflected his disbelief. The idea that she pictured him as cosmopolitan had obviously never occurred to him.

No, Ryan told himself. All the rough edges had been smoothed out, but deep within he was still the roughneck who had left the Georgian hills for Harvard. Young, intelligent but inexperienced in the ways of sophisticated people, he'd acted tough and cocky to hide the awful fear. The first year in Boston had been hell. He hadn't fit in at all. Cosmopolitan, be damned. He was just a damn good actor, that's all.

"Oh, Ryan. You think of me as a narrow person, unable to broaden her horizons. Maybe I have been. But the realization that I'll soon be thirty has made me slow down long enough to take a look at myself, at my life. Perhaps I'm ready for a change."

Her eyes entreated him to understand. His expression was still guarded, and her shoulders slumped in defeat. She closed her eyes, resting her forehead on her arms. She felt his hand on her hair, stroking gently, and held her breath.

"I wish..." he began softly. He didn't finish the statement.

Leave it for now, she told herself as she slid off the

bed and padded on bare feet to the closet for a robe. Let him think for a while about what she had revealed. He knew her so well. She only hoped he realized what the admission had cost from a former militantly independent woman.

"I'm hungry," she said quietly. She belted the robe and left the room without a glance at the man on the bed.

Ryan crossed his hands beneath his head, silent as he watched Rosemary leave the room. He knew what forces had driven her to the level of success she'd reached. He also knew where her priorities lay. Professionally there were few designers who could touch her talent. The awards she had received for her work were numerous and prestigious and were not given away on a whim. He knew and understood, because they were the same forces that had driven the young Ryan. He and Rosie were very much—too much—alike.

He believed sincerely that Rosemary's restlessness was a phase; like other phases it would pass. To some people the anniversary of thirty years was a milestone. As was forty—he frowned—he wasn't that far from forty himself. And fifty. Any birthday made you stop to take a look, either backward or forward, at your life, to see what you had accomplished or overlooked. But the year that marked each decade was an even more thought-provoking one.

Rosemary had acknowledged as much when she'd agreed to leave the city. With a groan he threw his legs over the edge of the mattress and sat up. Dammit to hell! What was he going to do? He could not, would not, let himself become vulnerable to this beautiful, remarkable and totally lovable woman. He wiped his face with a rough swipe of both hands and raked his fingers through his hair.

Ryan refused to admit to her that the feelings he'd had five years ago had returned, twice as strong, twice as dangerous. What he should do was send her back to New York. Hell, it galled him to admit that to himself.

A few minutes later Ryan joined Rosemary in the kitchen. She had switched on his mother's small radio, and the sound of country music drowned out all others. He reached out to lower the volume. "Honey?"

She turned that beautiful gaze, like a blue laser beam, on him. He saw hope there, and trust, and love. And he realized then that those three emotions were hard to kill.

"Maybe," he said.

10

THE PHONE RANG, dragging all three of them from a deep sleep. Settled comfortably on the pillow beside Ryan's head, Butch mewed in protest.

"I'll get it," Ryan said sleepily. Then, "Good Lord, Rosie! Look what time it is!" He sprang from the bed and headed for the parlor.

She passed him like a streak of lightning and grabbed for the telephone before he could answer. "Hello," she said breathlessly.

Ryan lifted an enquiring brow.

"Yes, I'm practically on my way." She shot Ryan an agitated look. The man on the other end of the line was clearly annoyed. Finally in desperation she blurted out, "I'm sorry, Charles. My alarm didn't go off this morning."

Dawning comprehension cleared Ryan's brow. He crossed his arms on a tall chair back and laughed silently, shaking his head at the weak, overused excuse. "Liar," he mouthed.

She stuck out her tongue at him. "Ryan? Why would I know where he is?" She listened for a moment, frowning. "Yes, if I do see him I'll be sure to tell him."

"Tell me what?" he said, coming out from behind the chair to gather her naked body into his arms.

"You can't sleep all night here anymore," was all she said.

"Good morning," he murmured against her lips.

"Good morning." She kissed him quickly and untangled herself. "This is a small town, and I'm living in your mother's house. Anyone could have driven by and seen your car."

"I'm afraid it's a little late for you to be worrying, honey." A trace of guilt warmed his face, however. He should have thought of that himself. It was unfair of him to subject Rosemary's reputation to gossip.

"I don't want to be a favorite topic for the rumor mill in Apple Valley, Ryan."

"You're learning fast," he said wryly. Then his brows came together in a black scowl. "That was the message?" He followed her back into the bedroom. "Did Charles imply..."

She reached for her robe. "No, but it will only be a matter of time before someone will. Then everyone will be talking."

A smile smoothed his expression into something resembling masculine satisfaction. He took the robe from her and held it for her to slip her arms into the sleeves. "They'll only be saying how lucky I am." He lifted the heavy fall of her hair from underneath her collar. "You can always tell Charles his boss has a special job only you can handle."

"Wouldn't he love that?" she said sarcastically. The small frown returned as she scooped up his clothes and handed them to him. "No. The message concerned Carole. Her mother is going into the hospital in Chattanooga. Carole's leaving this afternoon and would like to have a meeting with you before she goes."

He picked out his jeans and tossed the rest of the stack on the bed. "Poor kid," he said, shoving his legs into the denims. "Her mother has been sick off and on for years."

"I'm sorry. Does she have any other family?" In spite of her sympathy for her friend, Rosemary couldn't tear her eyes from his hands as he made himself comfortable in the jeans and zipped them. No underwear? She crossed her arms over her chest and let the bed post hold her up.

He snapped the fastener and picked up his shirt. "Two brothers. She won't be alone." His arms went into the short sleeves first; then he grabbed a handful of the knit fabric and dragged it over his head.

"Good." She swallowed hard when the muscles of his chest rippled under the light covering of hair, then were covered. "Would—could I get you some coffee before you go?"

Jamming the shirt into the waistband of his pants, he leaned over to give her a kiss on the cheek. "I'd better not wait, honey. I'll go home to shower and change and see you for lunch. Okay?"

Rosemary nodded. Who would have thought

that watching him put his clothes on was every bit as sexy as watching him take them off? He was completely unaware of the effect he had on her. Maybe it was better that way. She had already revealed far too much vulnerability where he was concerned. "Okay," she said weakly.

When he got to the bedroom door he turned. "Rosie?" he said very softly.

She met his teasing gaze. He gave her an exaggerated, outrageous wink. "You do the same thing to my libido," he said, and was gone. She picked up a pillow and threw it at the space where he had been. He was much too good at those parting shots.

"IT WON'T WORK, Rosemary. The colors are selected years in advance and coordinated with other fields of decorating."

"But, Charles, you've seen the effect other national and world events have had on the color predictions. They're only forecasts—they're not written in stone. Remember the last election year? When everyone was scrambling to fill the public demand for blues and reds? The predictions that year were for pastels, and primarily greens at that."

"That was for clothes," he pronounced grimly, looking for support from his staff. Everyone was suddenly very busy.

"Do you mean to tell me the election didn't have any effect on your market?" she demanded, fists planted on her hips. "The effect was certainly felt in other phases of decorating."

When Charles didn't answer she knew she was right. She just *knew* she was right on this. The thought that had been niggling at her had finally come to the surface as she was driving to the mill that morning. A voice on the radio had informed listeners that the president's three-week tour of the Orient—China, Japan and the Phillipines—had been expanded to include Korea. His departure was scheduled for late September, on the first day of autumn.

Rosemary had paused only long enough to pick up her mail at the reception desk before bearding the lion in his den. Charles hadn't liked her idea and had followed her back into the studio to continue the argument.

"It's too big a gamble," he said flatly now. "We have a reputation to consider."

A demand for chinoiserie—furniture, ceramics, fabrics and color, those beautifully vivid Oriental colors—would sweep the country; Rosemary was willing to bet her drawing pencil on it. And Ryan Mills would be ready. Better than ready—ahead of the field, out front, leading the way. "I have a reputation, too, Charles," she reminded him sharply.

Charles left on that note, retiring to his office, grumbling like a sore-headed bear. She grinned at the other members of the design staff, who had kept their faces buried in their various projects during the exchange and were now looking at her wide-eyed. "Does he always growl like that?" she asked no one in particular.

Sammy, a red-headed man barely as tall as Rosemary, answered for them. "Always," he said with a grin. "But you caught him out on that one. He should have thought of the Oriental influence. He prides himself on being way ahead of the market."

She swung to the bookshelves behind her. "Well, let's see what we can come up with here. Otherwise I'm going to have to find a library."

Sammy pointed out several volumes that featured Oriental color and design analysis, and she got right to work.

When the call came several hours later, summoning her to Ryan's office, Rosemary looked at the clock in surprise. It was well past lunchtime. Ryan was probably starved.

She pierced her chignon with the pencil and grabbed her purse. She hoped she could talk him into sending out for something. The creative juices were flowing, and she didn't want to stop, wouldn't have stopped for anyone else.

"You read my mind," she said when she entered to find one corner of his desk cleared off to make room for a giant-sized pizza and two cold bottles of beer.

"Did I? About what?" he asked as he took the purse from her shoulder, dropped it on the floor and took her in his arms. He had discarded his jacket. His shirt smelled of laundry starch, a crisp, clean smell that went well with the purely masculine scent of him. His slacks, as always, were tailored perfectly, yet her mind's eye replaced them with tight jeans, sans underwear. He covered her willing lips in a searing kiss.

"About that, too," she murmured, emerging from his embrace with a slightly dazed look in her huge blue eyes. "You have to stop doing that to me, Ryan. Especially at work," she mumbled, making an effort to regain control over her knees. But China, Japan *and* Korea were forgotten under the spell of his virility.

He laughed and held a chair out for her. "Honey, telling me to stop kissing those luscious lips is like telling me to stop breathing. Have some pizza." He reached to pull a slice free, deftly twisting his wrist so as not to lose any of the cheese.

She passed over the compliment, perhaps because it made her so happy, took a small piece and bit into it. "Mmm, Italian sausage. My favorite."

They ate in silence for a few minutes. The pizza was fresh and delicious, and Rosemary was surprised by her hunger.

At last Ryan leaned back in his chair, reaching for the brown bottle. He took a long draft and sighed. "Was your boss very mad at you for being late?"

She hesitated before she answered. "Not really. But I think he's angry about something else."

"What's that?" he asked idly, taking another swallow from the bottle.

She was always reluctant to explain her ideas until they were firmly fixed in her mind, but this was Ryan's business. She explained her reservations about the color predictions at length. Ryan peppered her with questions but was noncommittal when she asked if he thought she was right. "We'll have to see," was all he would say.

"HOLD THE DOOR OPEN, PAUL," Ryan muttered grimly. "I'll be right out."

"Yes, sir, Mr. Tarleton." The security guard tried unsuccessfully to hide a grin.

It was after midnight, and this was the third time Ryan had returned to the plant since the offices had closed for the day. And the last, he swore silently as he strode down the hall to the studio.

Rosemary was so engrossed in her work that his presence had barely registered those other times. She had eaten the sandwich he'd brought her at nine-thirty without even noticing that it was peanut butter, and when he'd informed her that he'd gone by the cottage to feed Butch, she had simply replied, "Good," without looking up.

"Okay, that's it," he pronounced as he walked into the brightly lit room.

She tossed the pencil carelessly on the board in front of her and lifted her hands over her head in a slow, catlike stretch. "Yes," she sighed, letting them fall again. "Lord, I'm tired. I can't do any more tonight, but I need to call New York first thing in the morning."

Ryan, who had been ready for an argument, smiled at her with an indulgent shake of his head. "Artist at work."

"What?"

"Do you know what time it is, honey?" He picked up her purse and handed it to her. Then with an arm around her waist he guided her out of the office, flipping off the lights as they left.

"No. Is it late?" She rested her head on his shoulder.

"It's after midnight," he said, his lips against her temple.

"Really?" Could it possibly be that late? "Oh, poor Butch. He must be starving."

Ryan gave her a strange look. Rosie threw herself into everything she did with equal enthusiasm. The idea made him pause to wonder if he could be wrong about her ability to adjust. Maybe it wouldn't be such a risk, after all, to think about them . . . together. He didn't allow the word "permanently" to end the thought, not yet. "I went by the cottage to feed Butch, and fed you, too. Don't you remember?"

"Sometimes I get carried away," she admitted meekly. "What did I eat?"

Laughing, he hugged her to him. "Peanut butter."

She yawned. "Good. I like peanut butter."

"Yes," he answered gently, "I know."

"I DON'T SUPPOSE you'd like to go camping next weekend?" Ryan asked the next morning over a breakfast he had prepared. Somehow they had both forgotten that he wasn't supposed to spend the night at the cottage.

Rosemary swallowed the wrong way, and a fit of coughing overcame her. "Camping?" Oh, Lord, what next?

"Carole had made reservations to camp on Cumberland Island off the coast of south Georgia. The park service restricts the number of permits for camping in order to protect the environment. One for this time of year is hard to come by. She hated to see it go to waste, so she offered it to me."

"I'd love it," she said when her throat cleared.

"C'mon, Rosie," he chided. "We both know you have no idea whether you'd love it or not."

Was Ryan testing her? She heard the cynicism in his voice and waited for a minute. "You're right. I don't know. What I meant was that I'd love to try."

"I don't understand why," Ryan said flatly.

She took a long breath and propped her chin on her hand. "Because I want to be with you," she said simply. "Ryan, you seem to have the impression that I spoke rashly when I said I loved you. I didn't. Don't you realize I have doubts, too? Not about how I feel, but about whether I'm really strong enough to grow if I'm uprooted. The only thing I know to do is gather all the information. And that means doing all the things you like."

"Even if you hate doing them? I saw how bored you were at the ball game, and the rafting trip was worse. You were thoroughly irked by the time it was over."

"I've never done anything like that before." She

stirred her coffee slowly, giving herself time to form an answer. "It wasn't too bad."

He eyed her suspiciously. "Are you telling me you enjoyed it?"

"No. I wouldn't want to lie to you. At the time I thought it was horrible." She sat up straighter. "But I survived," she said proudly.

Ryan watched her speculatively. "That meant a lot to you, didn't it? Testing yourself?"

It dawned on her that he was right. She had thought he was testing her, but she had really been testing herself, and far more stringently than he would. A smile lighted her eyes, spread across her face. "Yes, I suppose I am. And I'd love to try this. I'll survive a camping trip, too."

"All right, Rosie. Let's give it a whirl. We'll leave early Saturday morning."

"Let me be responsible for the food, Ryan." When she saw that he was about to object, she went on in a rush. "I'll consult with Zack if I can't do it myself, but please let me try." Ideas were already forming in her mind. She would make this a camping trip he'd never forget. Another thought, one not so welcome, intruded. "Ryan, do you know that Carole is very attracted to you?"

"Is she?" Ryan asked, hiding a smile. He did know that Carole would have liked more than a boss-employee relationship, but he'd never felt inclined to pursue that possibility.

"Yes. I just wondered if you knew." Her voice was subdued, and she wouldn't meet his eyes.

He looked down at her bent head. "Are you jealous, Rosie?"

She nodded, surprising him. "Oh, I'm not really jealous. Carole is a good friend, and I'm very fond of her. It's just that the two of you have so much in common."

In addition to being surprised, Ryan was inexplicably pleased by her reaction. Jealousy had never pleased him before. She was right about Carole, too, he noted. And wondered why he had never had the slightest romantic interest in someone who would have been so suited to his way of life. He was very much afraid, he admitted to himself wryly, that he'd never recovered from the brief, aborted attachment five years ago. "Rosie..." he began, then stopped, unsure of what he wanted to say.

Standing, Rosemary picked up her plate, staring down at the congealed mess of scrambled egg. He knew she didn't eat breakfast. "You wouldn't hesitate to take her along, would you?" she asked as she vigorously scraped the contents into the trash. "You'd have every confidence in her on a camping trip."

He got to his feet and circled the table to take her firmly in his arms. "Honey, I promise you that I have no romantic interest in Carole, and if she has any feelings for me they don't run deep. I've never thought of Carole as more than a friend, a buddy." His fingers cradled her face; he used his thumb to tilt her chin up. "Do you believe me?" he asked quietly.

After the night they had just shared, how could

Rosemary not believe him? She stretched on tiptoe to his lips. "Yes," she breathed. "Now you'd better go. And you still can't spend the night again."

"That's what you told me yesterday," he murmured huskily.

"But today I really mean it," she said, wrapping her arms tighter around him.

He groaned, his embrace forceful but tender, his mouth working over hers hungrily. Their passion was restrained by the knowledge that they had to leave for the plant shortly, and frustration sheared through them both.

"We'll have the weekend, but I'd like more than a weekend with you," Ryan said, nipping at her earlobe. "I'd like a long vacation somewhere without telephones, somewhere warm and isolated." He rested his forehead against hers.

"I'd like that, too." *We could have a lifetime*, she thought.

"Maybe we can manage a trip soon."

By Friday morning Rosemary had finished three of the four pattern designs she had planned for the Rosemary line. The color chart variations for all four had been done, as well. She knew she could complete design number four by that night and have her mind free for the weekend ahead, to concentrate solely on Ryan.

Her plans had been made and implemented for those two days on Cumberland Island. She was going to use every minute and every facet of the trip to convince Ryan that their two life-styles could merge effectively. She could hardly wait to see Ryan's face when he realized what she had accomplished. She had ordered all the food over the telephone from a store in Atlanta, and it had been delivered on Thursday by Greyhound bus. When she tried, Rosemary Addison could be as resourceful outside her element as in it. She had even bought blue jeans.

Assembling her materials, graph paper and tempera paints, she set to work. Next week she would do the silk screens, strike them in different colors and run the samples. Ordinarily this part of the process would have been left to someone else, but Rosemary wanted to carry the project through herself, from beginning to end.

A door opened and closed, a phone rang, a computer printer set up a clacking noise. Rosemary ignored all the sounds.

Charles appeared in the doorway to his office. "May I see you for a minute, Miss Addison?"

"Certainly, Mr. Davis," she answered with equal formality.

She entered with a smile on her face, which was suddenly frozen there when she saw the items spread on his desk. Her first design had not only been silk-screened, several cloth strikes had been made showing the design in various colors. She whirled on him.

"Where did you get my drawing?" she demanded.

"From your desk." He picked up one of the strikes, a square of cotton in a subdued version of Chinese red, suitable for floor covering and pretended to study the design dispassionately.

In spite of her agitation she couldn't help noticing that the design as well as the color were beautiful. "How dare you do this, Charles? You knew I wanted to prepare the screens myself."

He answered without a trace of emotion in his voice. "I am still ultimately responsible for product development at Ryan Mills. I wanted the marketing department to see them."

"I was supposed to be in on the presentation," she argued. "You took my design and showed it to them without giving me a chance to explain the reason for the color changes, didn't you?"

No one had ever treated her work in such a cavalier manner before. She was furious, but trying hard to hold on to her temper.

"Of course I explained to them your idea about the president's trip. The trouble is that they didn't seem impressed. If they don't think your ideas are salable, there's not much point in your continuing, is there?"

The hands at her sides clenched into impotent fists. "Have you told Ryan?"

"No. I'll leave that to the marketing boys. They'll prepare a memo." He tossed the cloth carelessly back on his desk.

"Ryan Mills is paying me a great deal of money. Aren't you worried about that?" she asked as her mind churned, seeking an excuse for his extraordinary behavior.

He was unmoved. "Not particularly. I'm sure marketing will point out that it's a small loss compared to what we would lose if we went ahead with production."

"Charles, why did you do this?" She asked the question quietly, when what she wanted to do was scream. "Why?"

Suddenly his face was suffused with an alarming amount of red color. "You think you can't make a mistake, Miss Hotshot New York Designer?" he sneered. "Well, our marketing people are some of the best in the business, and they don't agree."

She drew back, shocked by the genuine dislike she saw in his eyes. "But can't we discuss it with marketing? I can explain—"

He seemed to recover himself as he interrupted. "I don't explain myself to anyone," he said coldly.

Rosemary left the office as quickly as her shaking legs would take her, stumbling slightly at the threshold leading to the hall. Scenes like the one she'd just experienced were totally foreign to her. She had to pull herself together. Her agitation was sure to provoke questions if she returned to the studio in this condition. She headed for the haven of the ladies' room.

All the insecurities that plagued her whenever she began a new job came back in a flood, and on this occasion were magnified a thousand times, distorted by her feeling for Ryan. Maybe she was wrong. Maybe overriding the color predictions was too big a gamble. Who did she think she was to decide so arrogantly that she knew best?

Hotshot New York designer, indeed. She'd return the money, she decided suddenly. She'd think of some way out, for Ryan and for her. Concern for her was what had motivated Ryan to offer her the job, anyway. She couldn't allow Ryan Mills to lose money on this project. If marketing didn't believe there was value in her ideas, they must be worthless.

Splashing cold water on her cheeks, she dried them with rough paper towels. She needed to see Ryan, needed to warn him before the memo from marketing arrived. Maybe it already had.

Whirling, she left the room and headed directly for his office.

"Hey." Jackie greeted her with a smile and replaced the telephone receiver. "I was just trying to reach you."

"Jackie, I have to see Ryan," Rosemary explained breathlessly, ignoring protocol as she opened the door to his office. It was empty.

"He just left. He had to go to Atlanta unexpectedly, Rosie."

"Atlanta?" Rosemary said blankly.

"The Merchandise Mart. Some problem with the new showroom. Since he's leaving for this vacation, he wanted to take care of it before he left."

"Vacation?" She needed him. And he'd gone on a vacation!

Jackie glanced down at a pad on the desk before her. She placed a check mark beside each item as she relayed the messages. "He said to tell you he'll probably be very late getting back tonight. You're not to worry about the kitten, I'll keep it while you're gone, and he said to meet him at the airport in the morning at six."

"Airport?"

The older woman finally realized something was wrong. She rose and came around the desk. "What's the matter, Rosie?" she said, automatically using Ryan's pet name for her.

Rosemary's eyes flooded, but she swallowed the tears. "I've just had a blowup with Charles. It was a dilly."

Gently Jackie led Rosemary to a chair, hesitating before she spoke. "Charles is terrified of you."

"What?" Rosemary's head came up sharply.

Jackie nodded. "He's a very insecure man. He thinks you're after his job."

"That's ridiculous! I'm not!"

"Of course you're not. But everyone knows that you and Ryan are...close."

For "close," read "sleeping together," thought Rosemary dispiritedly.

Jackie went on talking in her calm, unruffled tone. "Charles thinks that if you marry, Ryan will have no need for him anymore."

All the indignation went out of Rosemary at the words. Poor Charles, always the pessimist, always worrying about what might not happen. In this case what *would* not happen. She laughed, a hollow sound even to her own ears. "Ryan and I will never marry," she said dully.

Jackie's speculative attitude was obvious, but she didn't ask any questions. Instead she said lightly, "I'm glad the two of you are taking this trip. Ryan told me how hard you've been working, and he always works too hard. It will do you both good to get away."

Trip? Oh, Lord, yes. The camping trip had been erased from her mind by Charles's revelations. Rosemary smiled up at the woman who still hovered protectively at her side. "I'll be at the airport at six, Jackie. But I...I need to go home early today. Do you think that will be all right?"

"Of course. Rosie, are you sure you're okay?"

Rosemary stood up. "I'm fine." She was proud that her voice was again under control. "I'll see you on Monday."

"On Monday? But I thought Ryan had planned..." Jackie's voice trailed off as Rosemary walked out of the office without a backward glance.

CROSSING HER ARMS protectively across her midriff, Rosemary stared vacantly through the window into the moon-drenched night. Butch drifted around her ankles, offering support and comfort, which was totally ignored. When he began to sink his tiny claws into the blue chiffon of her nightgown she relented, scooping up the little black body to cuddle him under her chin.

She had placated her fears by promising to face them tomorrow when there was some chance of a solution. Tonight, nothing could be done. Tomorrow, she had several choices.

Her job was over in Apple Valley; now all she had to do was tell Ryan. Obviously he hadn't received the memo from the marketing department. If he had he would have come storming into the studio and demanded to be told how in the hell she had managed to mess up so royally.

Damn Charles, anyway! His timing was atrocious. Now the burden of confession was on her shoulders, for she couldn't possibly pretend for two days that everything was all right.

Ryan would be so disappointed in her. That hurt worse than any of the rest. She buried her nose in the fur of Butch's soft, warm body, and he squeaked in protest at being held so tightly. She stooped to let him down.

Restlessly she turned, and her eyes fell on the stamped envelope on the breakfast table, ready to mail in answer to a letter she'd received today, a letter from France. She wandered over to pick it up. Deep in thought, she tapped the envelope against her thumbnail.

Also on the table was the backpack Ryan had brought over. The lightweight nylon bundle was filled to capacity. She had staggered under its weight when she hefted it to the table, but she was sure that when it was in place on her shoulders, she would be able to manage.

Now all that remained was to get a good night's sleep in preparation for the trip. She walked out of the room, flipping off the switch as she went.

11

THE PILOT WATCHED HER STRUGGLE with the bulky pack for only an instant before he responded, striding across the grass to the parking area to take it from her. "This thing's really heavy, Miss Addison. Are you sure you can manage?"

Despite the coolness of the dawn, she was perspiring with the effort, though she denied any qualms. "Sure, Stan. I'm stronger than I look." She pushed down the lock on the car door and slammed it shut. "Ryan isn't here yet?"

The man glanced at his watch. "Any minute now. He's never late."

Sure enough, the words were hardly out of his mouth when the dusty Lincoln turned into the airport parking lot, illuminating them both in its headlights. Ryan got out, grinning from ear to ear. "Good morning! It's a great day for a camping trip," he said exuberantly, and Rosemary's spirits took a nose dive. He was so excited, like a young boy. She hated to pierce his good mood with her gloomy one. She couldn't.

Forcing a smile to her lips and a spring to her step, she circled her car and went to meet him.

"How do you like my outfit?" she asked, pirouetting in front of him and ending up in his arms for a hug.

Ryan held her away for an instant, his hands on her shoulders, while his smoky eyes wandered over her jeans and red gingham shirt. Despite the boyish cut of the jeans, her femininity and sensuality were so obvious his heart took a leap. Her eyes shone blue in the early-morning light, and her black hair was brushed and tied back in a bright red scarf. Still he kept returning to that gingham shirt. It, too, was cut in a boyish style. Her breasts strained the metal snaps. "You look great in jeans," he murmured huskily. "I knew you would."

Rosemary grinned at the compliment, because his eyes weren't on the jeans. She was unprepared for the sudden, almost uncontrollable desire that rose in her, stimulating her nipples and warming the spot deep within that only he could touch. She leaned toward him, his name an indistinct whisper on her parted lips. Finally he tightened his arms and claimed her mouth in a thorough kiss. He tasted of toothpaste and fine, rich coffee.

"I missed you last night," he murmured, too low for Stan's ears.

"I missed you, too," she murmured back. "I didn't sleep very well."

"That's good to hear." He grinned and kissed her again. "Come on. Let's get moving. I want to make the nine-fifteen ferry."

Ryan strapped Rosemary into her seat before

joining Stan in the co-pilot's seat. Relieved that her confession could wait a bit longer, she settled into the plush upholstery and closed her eyes. When she had told him she hadn't slept well, it had been a gross understatement. She hadn't closed her eyes until after three, and the alarm had gone off at five.

THEY LANDED at the Brunswick Airport to find a rental car ready and waiting. While Ryan signed the insurance papers Stan loaded the backpacks into the trunk of the conservative blue sedan.

"Whew!" he declared again. "That *is* heavy. What on earth do you have in there, Miss Addison?"

"Shhh," she cautioned, looking over her shoulder at Ryan. He didn't seem to have heard. "I brought something special for dinner tonight." She grinned. "So I won't have to carry the extra weight back if our boss is just hungry enough."

Stan shook his head, chuckling dryly. "If you'll excuse me for saying so, he's going to have to have the appetite of an elephant."

"Why?" asked Ryan, coming up behind them.

"Never mind," said Rosemary hastily. "Have a nice trip, Stan."

Ryan waved him off and came around to join her in the front seat. "What were you talking about?"

"It's something special. And that's all I'm going to say about it. Now how far is it to St. Mary's?" she asked casually, hoping to divert him.

"Rosemary?"

"All right." She gave in with a good-natured grumble. "Stan thinks my backpack is too heavy." Quickly she added, "It isn't. I tried it out myself, and I can manage."

"Are you sure?"

"I'm sure," she said staunchly. "How far is it to St. Mary's?"

"Less than an hour," he told her with a tender smile, reaching for her hand. "But far too long for you to be so far away from me. Come over here."

She complied, tucking her shoulder behind his while he drove.

"You can take a nap if you like," he offered.

"I'm not sleepy." It was true at that moment. When she remembered the reason for her insomnia she knew a brief qualm, but shrugged it off. The exciting prospect of two whole days alone with Ryan was enough to banish worry and weariness.

Although they talked of inconsequential things for most of the journey, even the silences were warm with promise. Ryan was different today somehow, more relaxed and happier than she'd ever seen him. He kept grinning down at her for no reason, acting like someone with a surprise.

She had a surprise, too, Rosemary thought, pleased at the picture that came to mind. Then she sobered. She had two surprises—he wasn't going to like the one Charles had sprung on her yesterday.

"Anything happen yesterday at the plant?" was his uncanny question. "Did you finish your last design?"

She glanced out the window in time to see a sign announcing that they were inside the St. Mary's city limits. "Well, no, not quite," she said in a low voice, and wondered if he heard the sudden strain and nervousness that made her hoarse. "I'm afraid there's a problem."

"Nothing we can't solve, I'm sure." Ryan checked his watch. "We're early. Let's have some coffee." He wheeled the car into the gravel parking lot in front of a white frame building, that bore the sign Café.

When the waitress had taken their orders, again he reached for her hand. "Now tell me what's bothering you, honey."

She tried to be absolutely dispassionate as she repeated the conversation with Charles. But even leaving out the unpleasant things, she saw the thundercloud growing in his expression. He was furious. The muscle in his jaw clenched and relaxed more than once during her recital. Shifting uncomfortably in the chair, she berated herself for being so adamant with Charles. She could have done some nice designs using the color predictions and avoided this confrontation.

No. That wouldn't have worked at all. It wasn't in her nature to settle for the merely acceptable. She had to give her best to a job or she couldn't live with herself. If that made Ryan angry, so be it.

"Rosie—" His voice was rough.

"No, Ryan. Before you say anything let me add something. I don't want you to feel responsible for me. I know that the only reason you brought me

South was because you thought I needed to get away." She waved a hand, palm up, and he reached for it.

"That wasn't the only reason," he said quietly but fiercely, gripping her fingers.

"I won't hold you to the contract, Ryan. I—" She broke off when the waitress returned to set two cups of coffee in front of them. "All I can do is apologize, and leave and tell you that I'll return the advance."

"Apologize? Is that what you think I want?" His control was more intimidating than an eruption of temper would have been. "Don't you think that since I own the damn plant, I should have a chance to voice my opinion? I'm angry at Charles, not you." He regarded her speculatively, then released her hand as though it burned him. All his misgivings returned in a rush. "But I guess it's a good thing I found out that you're ready to run back to New York at the first sign of trouble."

She caught her breath and searched his features; his face was a mask of indifference. "I'm not running," she answered quietly, successfully covering her own hurt.

"That's what I'd call it," he bit out.

Slowly, filling the immense need to hide her vulnerability, a smoldering anger came to her rescue. Rosemary knew she had a temper, and she decided she deserved a so-called artistic tantrum now. Fury surged through her, growing, swelling. The memory of all the irritating obstacles she'd had to overcome to live in Georgia mounted one on top of the other, until they filled her very being, crowding out all reason.

"I am not running," she repeated with quiet but raging resentment. "Don't you dare accuse me of that again. Your *precious*—" she spat the word at him "—vice-president of design, or product development, or whatever you call him, told me I wasn't wanted. That my designs wouldn't sell. My work wasn't good enough for him! He called me a hotshot New York designer!" She slapped the table between them with the flat palm of her hand.

The sound went through the diner like the crack of a rifle. Heads turned to watch.

Ryan, whose own anger had faded when faced with the storm of hers, made a terrible mistake. He chuckled under his breath.

Rosemary inhaled long and deeply, oblivious to the interest of those around them. "What the *hell* are you laughing about?"

"I—I'm sorry, but you're so...so indignant! Like a little banty hen whose rooster has pecked her tail feathers." He went off into whoops of laughter.

Rosemary didn't think his remark funny at all, but with all the calm she could muster she straightened her shoulders and fixed him with a glare of pure disdain for his humor. "I've had an offer from a French company wanting me to design bedding for the top of their line. The letter came yesterday. Luxury fabrics, special laces, worldwide marketing—it's a very flattering offer."

His laughter was cut short. For a full minute he studied her thoughtfully and silently. "You mean you're actually considering the offer?" he asked quietly.

She nodded. "I'm thinking it over."

"Tell me something, Rosie," he said after another minute. "If you knew all this, why did you come with me this weekend?"

"I wish I hadn't come. Believe it or not, it's not that easy to leave you. I'd like to go home."

"Which home?" he asked softly.

Rosemary wanted to howl. She wanted to bury her face in her arms and cry until there were no more tears left. But she didn't. "My own home," she said, and added so he wouldn't be confused, "In New York."

Ryan's slight show of tenderness vanished at her statement. The color seemed to drain from his face.

They stared at each other, both realizing they had reached a turning point in their relationship. What happened in the next few seconds would determine where they went from there.

"Too bad," Ryan snapped at last. "You're stuck. I gave Stan the rest of the weekend off. He's gone to visit his girlfriend's parents in central Florida. Sorry," he added in an offhand manner.

He didn't sound sorry at all, she thought. He sounded like the night manager of a dungeon, ready to start torturing his next victim.

"Anyone in here taking the ferry to Cumberland?" The voice interrupted their hostilities. Both their heads came around to glare at the wiry man with the gray hair and squinty blue eyes. "We'll be leaving in five minutes," he told the restaurant at large.

"Let's go," said Ryan as he reached into his pocket. He tossed a bill and some change on the table. "Unless you're afraid. If you are, there's a motel next door."

"I'm not afraid. Not of anything," she told him haughtily, and rose to lead the way.

When Ryan lifted their packs out of the trunk he parroted Stan's comments. "Good Lord, Rosemary, what have you got in here? You'll never be able to carry this!"

"Your concern is touching," she said with a sneer. "Don't worry about me. I'm perfectly capable of managing. Would you like me to carry it to the boat?" she asked with saccharine sweetness. "To prove that I can?"

"You'd better save your energy," he retorted.

The ferry trip took only forty-five minutes, hardly long enough to cool two raging tempers. The small boat was crowded. She sat under the awning, stewing; he sat in the sun, baking.

And so Ryan didn't see her get off at Dungeness Landing until it was almost too late. "Rosemary!" He grabbed his pack and jumped off the ferry a second before it left the dock.

She was standing there staring around her, looking as lost as could be. Only a few people had disembarked there, because that was the dock for day visitors only. Campers stayed on the ferry until it reached the Sea Camp dock.

"You little fool!" Ryan erupted again. "You got off at the wrong place. You've just added another mile to your hike."

Oh, no. Rosemary's exhaustion, intensified by the disastrous argument, was beginning to catch up with her; she hid her uncertainty under a flippant answer. "Sorry," she said shortly. But when she'd first gotten off the boat and searched the faces around her, to find that Ryan's was not among them, she had known a frightening moment of loss and desolation, a preview of what was to come in a life without him.

He studied her flushed face from under narrowed lids, then shrugged. "We'll swap packs," he said mildly. "Even with the tent, mine is lighter."

"No," she proclaimed with the force of her fast-fading anger. "I packed it, I'll carry it."

"Rosie, be reasonable," he ordered impatiently.

She set her chin at an obstinate angle. "Will you help me put it on?"

The stubborn little mule hated to ask for any kind of help, thought Ryan, so he sighed and lifted the pack to arrange the straps over her shoulders. The curve of her cheek, the graceful stem of her neck, the tiny blue vein that throbbed at her temple were so delicate, so fragile. But her will was iron, and he felt his respect for her determination go up another notch.

That isn't so bad, thought Rosemary. Then Ryan

took his hands away, releasing the full weight. Her knees buckled, and she found herself on all fours in the sand, shaking her head in confusion, wondering how on earth she had gotten there. She felt like a turtle with its house on its back—no, what she really felt like was a fool. She was grateful that the other people who had disembarked from the boat were gone.

Two hands at her waist lifted her like a sack of grain and set her on her feet. "Dammit, Rosie! This is ridiculous." Ryan started to fuss with the straps.

"No! I can do it!" she shouted. "I can. I know I can," she finished faintly, taking one step on wobbly knees.

He grabbed her shoulders and shook her, pack and all. "Would it be so terrible to accept my help? Do you think you would be giving up your damned independence if I carried the damned pack?" The expression in his eyes was more than angry now. It was pained, a deep, gut-wrenching pain. Rosemary wanted to turn away from the sight, yet she couldn't. His pain hurt worse than her own. "Ryan..."

"What?" he almost shouted.

"Yes," she gasped.

"Yes, what?"

"Yes, would you help me, please?"

AN HOUR LATER Rosemary was drenched to her underwear in sweat—not perspiration, but healthy, smelly sweat. She slapped ineffectually at something that buzzed relentlessly around her face. Why, in God's name, did people *do* this? She could see nothing fun about having to stop to pick a seed tick off her neck. Lunch at the Russian Tea Room was fun. An opening night on Broadway was fun. Tramping through the woods, getting blisters on your feet was *not* fun.

"We're almost there." Ryan glanced over his shoulder at the pitiful figure behind him. He had to give her credit; she hadn't complained once. He faced the trail in front of him and grinned reluctantly. Rosie never gave up on anything.

The grin was replaced by a frown as he speculated on the story she'd told him about Charles. As Charles's employer, he was well aware of the man's personality quirks. His lack of self-confidence might explain the trick he'd pulled, but it certainly didn't excuse it. Ryan was going to have to have a long talk with Charles when he got home.

But why would Rosemary give in to the other designer? Why, indeed, he thought grimly. She probably wanted to take the job with the French company and was using the dispute with Charles as a way out of her contract. Ryan's mouth hardened in resolve. He wouldn't let her out. If the designs were unsalable, and he doubted that, she would just have to do them over again. She wasn't getting away from him this time.

Ryan had been dimly aware of a deep, rumbling sound, muffled by the dense oak forests that the trail wandered through. Suddenly from behind him he heard two screams—one animal, one definitely human. He whipped around, in a dead run before he finished the turn. Rosemary had fallen behind, and it took him harrowing seconds to reach her, throw an arm around her waist and drag her with him into the shelter of a tree.

She was shaking like a leaf and in no mood to appreciate the beauty of the thirty or so wild horses that thundered by, so he just held her.

The stallion that led them had probably emitted the scream, more of a warning to get out of the way than a threat. As Ryan watched, awed as always by the magnificent sight, the stallion dropped back to nip the hindquarters of a mare that was dawdling.

The horse caught the eye of the man for a fleeting instant, then gave a snort and galloped away. "See," the animal seemed to say. "That's how you handle females."

Ryan grinned at the spot where the animal had been. With a sudden lightening of his spirits he imagined. Rosie's reaction if he bit her bottom and told her to hurry.

From the protection of Ryan's arms, she had watched the last of the horses disappear through the forest. Their beauty and freedom were an impressive sight, but the scream from the horse in the lead had scared her out of several years' growth.

"Ready?" Ryan asked gently as he released her. "It's only a couple of hundred yards now."

His anger seemed to have completely evaporated, but she was wary of speaking. She nodded and set off once again in his wake.

The site was almost filled; still Ryan managed to find them a spot off to the side, away from most of the other campers. After he helped her off with her pack, she sank to the ground in relief. He came down beside her, sitting cross-legged. His tone when he spoke was reassuring, quieting her nerves with simple information.

"This is one of the developed campsites, so there are bathrooms and showers."

Thank goodness for small favors.

"We also have drinking water and can build a fire here, which we couldn't have done at a primitive campsite."

Rosemary shuddered, thinking for the first time that the situation might have been worse.

Ryan lifted an arm to point to a wall of sand thirty yards or so from where they sat. The sand was dotted with graceful, waving plumes of sawgrass. "The dunes protect the land from erosion. That means we can't see the ocean from here, but we can hear it. Listen."

Rosemary listened. A smile played across her lips. She nodded.

"Good girl." He gripped her shoulder in a way that was more appreciative than amorous, but it warmed her.

Rubbing his hands together in anticipation, he stood up in one fluid movement. "Now...I'll get started on the tent."

She scrambled to her feet, too. "Wouldn't you rather eat first? I packed some sandwiches on top, in case."

"That was a good idea. Actually, I'm starved. I skipped breakfast." He reached behind her for his pack. "I'll go fill up the canteens while you dig the sandwiches out."

She watched him go, feeling better by the minute. They were still treading lightly with each other, conversing like polite strangers and careful not to touch a raw spot, but the tension in the atmosphere had eased. Her vision blurred remembering the hurtful wounds each of them had inflicted with their anger.

Throwing off the depression before it could take hold, Rosemary unzipped the pack and took out the plastic box that kept the sandwiches fresh and square. If there was one thing she couldn't stand it was a sandwich bent out of shape.

She rezipped the pack. Until it was time for dinner she didn't want to reveal the surprise.

They ate their sandwiches, washed down with clear, pure water, and strolled for a while on the beach beyond the dunes. Ryan pointed out the tracks of the cotton mouse and rabbits among the sea oats. He showed her the holes of different diameters, which were homes for the ghost crabs.

"Why do they call them ghost crabs?" she asked, stopping to roll up the legs of her jeans.

He looked down at her bent head, catching a glimpse of her nape when the heavy fall of hair swung forward. "Mmm?"

She straightened and smiled. "I said, why do they call them ghost crabs?"

Unable to keep from touching her in some way,

he took her hand in a light grasp, and they continued their ambling walk. "Watch the shoreline," he told her.

Seeing the tiny creature, she laughed in delight. The shape of the crab was unmistakable, as was its shuffling, sideways gait. But the sandy color, blending in perfectly with the surroundings, soon made the crab shape hard to discern. If the crab hadn't been so quick it would have been easy to step on.

"Kit! Kit!" Rosemary's head swiveled toward the sound. A scolding bevy of terns rose from the edge of the dunes. Screaming and diving, they effectively routed a nosy raccoon, who scurried back into the protection of the forest. "They're so small. Are they young birds?" she asked.

"No, they're fully grown, just the smallest of the species, called the 'least' tern. They're threatened with extinction."

His voice held a husky sadness, revealing yet another facet of Ryan Tarleton, a man who cared about his environment and the creatures that shared it.

The sun had passed its summit before they returned to the campsite. "Would you like to have a shower while I set up the tent?"

"Are you trying to tell me something?" she teased, sniffing her shirt and screwing up her nose.

He lifted the hand he still held. "I think you smell pretty good. Like warm sunshine and sea breezes."

She caught her breath and looked up at him, willing him to go on, to bring back the feelings they had shared. If only he would take her in his arms, if only he would hold her, kiss her, reassure her...

But he didn't say more. His eyes were hooded, the long lashes effectively hiding his expression.

"A shower sounds wonderful," she said, finally disentangling her fingers. She turned away and walked over to her pack, swallowing hard against the burning sensation in her throat.

THE SHOWER, instead of raising her spirits, seemed to drain the remaining energy from her system. Sorrow weighed heavily on her. Dragging a clean pair of new, stiff jeans over her hips was a monumental task. Snapping the fresh blouse, which was the color of lemons, took a good five minutes. Putting one sneaker in front of the other as she walked back toward the campsite required all her concentration.

Conversely, Ryan was in a disgustingly energetic mood. "I'm getting hungry again. What are we having for supper?"

Rosemary blinked and almost groaned aloud. She had had such wonderful plans for dinner, and now she didn't give a damn. All she wanted to do was crawl into that welcoming tent and rest. She couldn't, though. The meal was her responsibility.

Ryan didn't notice her mood. He was rattling on and on, something about having a shower himself and about firewood. "Yes, all right. You go and gather wood, and I'll unpack everything," she mumbled.

"Rosie!"

Her head jerked upward.

He tilted up her chin, looking concerned. "I said do you need me to start the fire before I take a shower? What are we having?"

Her head was beginning to hurt from all the shouting. She forced herself to concentrate. "What we're having doesn't need to be cooked. You can build the fire later."

"Honey, are you all right?"

She spread her lips in a grimace that she hoped would pass for a smile. "I'm fine," she lied.

RYAN RETURNED SHORTLY—to stand staring in shocked amazement at the scene laid out before him. It took him several minutes to recover, and when he did he began to chuckle. The chuckle grew to unreserved laughter, the laughter to unrestrained shouts of hilarity, mixed with a few tears. He wiped his streaming eyes and let them roam over the campsite.

A spotless white damask cloth was spread on the ground; centered on it was one shining silver candle stick. A tall taper burned, flickering brightly despite the fact that it was still broad daylight. The sand flies were having a ball around a bowl filled with fresh strawberries and nectarines.

Rosemary must have cut the loaf of sourdough bread in half to make it fit in her pack. Now one piece rested on each china plate. At least she'd had sense enough to bring a tin of whipped cream cheese instead of butter, or they would have had a melted mess. Two bottles of wine balanced precariously in a plastic bucket. Thank God she hadn't packed the silver wine cooler. He would never have made it down the trail with that on his back.

Ryan stepped closer and, hunkering down, picked up another tin—all those cans accounted for the weight of the pack—to turn it over in his palm. What he saw almost did him in again. Pâté! Good Lord, she had brought liver pâté on a camping trip!

Shaking his head in wonder, he dropped his gaze to the first thing he'd seen when he returned to the campsite. Before the cloth or the candle, before the fruit or the wine or the pâté, what had sent him off into peals of laughter was Rosemary—lying flat on her back inside the tent, her arms flung out straight from her sides, wearing a slinky, satin nightshirt that left little to the imagination—and snoring softly.

"God, I love you, Rosemary Addison," he whispered.

ROSEMARY DIDN'T KNOW what woke her, maybe an unfamiliar sound. But she lifted her lids partway, to look drowsily through her lashes. Suddenly they flew open. Her head jerked up. When she took in the remnants of last night's feast, she let out a low groan and turned to bury her face in Ryan's neck.

Ryan? She groaned again. What must he have

thought? That she was certifiably insane? She had planned to explain the reasons for preparing the frivolous picnic; instead she had passed out without even the benefit of a glass of wine.

She had wanted to tell him that because she was a bit of a romantic and he enjoyed the great outdoors, she had thought they could mix the two. They would have laughed together and made love, and maybe, just maybe, the night could have produced miracles.

But Charles had intruded into her fantasy, and the French company and the fifty-pound albatross of a pack. Still something might have been salvaged after their walk on the beach. Until she had laid down to rest and wait for Ryan to come back. That was the last thing she remembered.

Now she was wrapped in his arms inside a sleeping bag, with no memory of how she'd gotten there. Tentatively she moved away enough to look at his face. And was startled to find herself fixed by a smoky gaze. "You're awake," she said unnecessarily.

One side of his mouth moved in the beginnings of a smile. "It's hard to sleep with a sexy lady wiggling around in the sleeping bag with you," he explained in a husky, early-morning voice.

They spoke together.

"Ryan, I..."

"Rosie, I..."

Ryan covered her lips with the tips of his fingers. "Let me go first, because my question is the most

important thing in the world to me right now—
Will you marry me?"

Her deep-blue eyes widened and shimmered
with tears. "But..." she mumbled under the light
pressure of his fingers.

"Everything else can be worked out. *Everything.* I
just want— *need—*" the word was wrung from him
"—to know the answer to that question."

She nodded vigorously.

"I love you," he whispered just before he took
her mouth with infinite care.

Rosemary struggled to free her arms from the
sleeping bag, bringing them together around his
neck.

And so when he raised up to lower the flap on
the tent, he had to take her clinging body with him
to do it. She covered his face with kisses and would
have asked a thousand questions had he not silenced her most effectively by making slow, lan-
guorous love to her. Twice.

He left the tent long enough between times to
poke up the fire and make coffee.

When he returned to her she stretched against
him and sighed. "I could stay right here all day."

He laughed softly. "Believe me, you couldn't,
honey. In an hour or so this tent is going to be hot
as hell."

"I know. I'm already feeling sticky."

As he pressed his lips to her forehead she felt
him smile. "That's from the insect repellant I
sprayed all over you last night."

"All over me?"

He drawled his answer, and his eyes took on a gleam of lazy enjoyment. "All-l-l over you."

"Thank you," she said formally.

"My pleasure." He took a swallow of his coffee and looked down into it, swirling the dark liquid slightly. When his gaze lifted to meet hers, the gray eyes seemed to have absorbed all the steam rising from the cup. "I love you. I've never stopped, I know that now."

"And I've finally come to my senses after five years. I love you, too, my darling." Her voice was husky with the memory of their lovemaking.

"I was afraid, Rosie, afraid to trust my heart to you a second time. But you've taught me things about love that I never knew. Things like not giving up when the odds are against you. Maybe if I hadn't given up so quickly five years ago..."

"No, Ryan," she said earnestly. She emptied the remains of the coffee and tossed the metal cup aside. On her knees, she faced him squarely, taking his face between her palms. Her voice was very soft, very sincere. "You were right when you said what we have now is better. Five years ago wasn't the right time for us." Leaning forward, she placed a tender kiss on his mouth, a kiss that was like a promise of forever.

His arm snaked around her waist to bring her back into his embrace. "Rosie, about this French offer."

"What did you have in mind?" she asked with a

leer. Laughing, knowing what he really meant, she pulled free one last time and rolled over to search in her pack. She came up with the envelope that had been on her kitchen table. It bore the address of the company.

He lifted an enquiring brow.

"Go on, open it," she urged. "I didn't mail it because I didn't know how many stamps to use."

Setting down his cup in the sand, Ryan tore open the envelope and silently read the letter. "Why did you let me think you'd accepted?" he asked quietly, some of the pain he'd felt lingering in his voice. The hand holding the piece of paper fell to his lap. "Do you know what it did to me to think you could so easily walk away from what we have?"

Rosemary caught her lower lip between her teeth and lifted her fingers to trace over his lips. "No, I didn't know, Ryan. You never told me. In fact, you kept saying that if you ever found yourself falling in love with me, you would fight the feeling."

He looked into her eyes for a long while. What she read in his heated her blood. "I suppose you're going to throw every stupid thing I ever said back at me," he accused unsteadily.

"Probably," she said with a loving smile. "If you give me trouble."

Ryan twisted to rummage in his own pack. He turned back to her with a closed fist, which he held out to her. Slowly he uncurled his fingers. In his palm lay a sparkling sapphire, set in white gold and surrounded by diamonds.

Rosemary clasped her hands under her chin and met his eyes. "You had this all the time?"

"I had planned to give it to you last night. Then we had what must have been the granddaddy of all fights. I thought I had lost you for good." He slipped the ring onto her finger, sealing it there with a kiss on her knuckle. "I've arranged to be away from the plant for a week. Stan will be back to fly us to Vegas this afternoon if you decide that you'll marry me."

"If I— Surely you knew, Ryan?" she whispered in disbelief. "Surely you knew that I would marry you?"

"Not until we walked the beach. I thought you'd decided that Paris held more appeal than Apple Valley. But on the beach you seemed content...and happy. I began to hope again."

Exuberantly she threw her arms around his neck. He held her so tightly that she could barely breathe. "And then I fell asleep in the middle of my big seduction scene," she said with a moan.

"And snored."

She pulled back. "I did not!"

That wonderful, teasing light appeared in his eyes. "You did," he swore, making an X over his heart. "I almost changed my mind at that, I tell you. The thought of spending my life with—"

Rosemary launched herself at him, the rest of the words were lost under her kiss.

Not until the plane was over the Mississippi River on the way to Nevada did Rosemary realize she had nothing to wear to her own wedding except jeans. And she didn't even care.

ANNE MATHER

Anne Mather, one of Harlequin's leading
romance authors, has published more
than 100 million copies worldwide,
including **Wild Concerto,**
a *New York Times* best-seller.

Catherine Loring was an
innocent in a South
American country beset by
civil war. Doctor Armand
Alvares was arrogant
yet compassionate.
They could not ignore
the flame of love igniting
within them...whatever
the cost.

HIDDEN IN THE FLAME

Available at your favorite bookstore in June, or send your name, address and zip or
postal code, along with a check or money order for $4.25 (includes 75¢ for postage and
handling) payable to Worldwide Library Reader Service to:

Worldwide Library Reader Service

In the U.S.
Box 52040
Phoenix, AZ
85072-2040

In Canada
5170 Yonge Street, P.O. Box 2800,
Postal Station A
Willowdale, Ont. M2N 6J3

HIF-A-1

You're invited to accept 4 books and a surprise gift **Free!**

Acceptance Card

Mail to: **Harlequin Reader Service®**

In the U.S.
2504 West Southern Ave.
Tempe, AZ 85282

In Canada
P.O. Box 2800, Postal Station A
5170 Yonge Street
Willowdale, Ontario M2N 6J3

YES! Please send me 4 free Harlequin Temptation® novels and my free surprise gift. Then send me 4 brand new novels every month as they come off the presses. Bill me at the low price of $1.99 each ($1.95 in Canada)—a 13% saving off the retail price. There are no shipping, handling or other hidden costs. There is no minimum number of books I must purchase. I can always return a shipment and cancel at any time. Even if I never buy another book from Harlequin, the 4 free novels and the surprise gift are mine to keep forever.

142 BPX-BPGE

_____
Name   (PLEASE PRINT)

_____
Address   Apt. No.

_____
City   State/Prov.   Zip/Postal Code

This offer is limited to one order per household and not valid to present subscribers. Price is subject to change.   ACHT-SUB-1